LETTER TO LORENZO

AMANDA PRANTERA

BLOOMSBURY

To PIETRO

Published by Bloomsbury, New York and London.
Distributed to the trade by St. Martin's Press

A CIP catalogue record for this book
is available from the Library of Congress

ISBN 1-58234-018-8

Published in Great Britain 1999 by Bloomsbury Publishing Plc.

First U.S. Edition 1999
10 9 8 7 6 5 4 3 2 1

Typeset in Great Britain by Hewer Text Ltd, Scotland
Printed in the United States of America by RR Donnelley & Sons,
Harrisonburg, Virginia

B+T 7/99
14.47

CHAPTER ONE

Begin with a bang. The bang. An unnatural end but a natural enough beginning. Especially, as I suppose it must be, if it is for Lorenzo's shattered ears, deaf for ever, that I principally intend this story. The bang with which his life stopped and mine . . . Well, if I could find a simple verb to sum up the effects it had on mine, then that would be that and I wouldn't have to tell the story.

It was late at night when the news reached me. Or latish anyway: it couldn't have been *that* late because when I left the bed to answer the telephone and saw Lorenzo's empty place and undented pillow I wasn't worried, made no connection, merely thought he had come back, found me asleep, and was sitting next door in his study, too immersed in his work to answer. In fact it took me an incredibly long time to understand what I was being told – a fact which shamed me afterwards, I don't know why. On the other end of the line was Marini, the one-time foreman who now looked after the office side of things and did odd jobs for Elvira as well, like running her to the airport and . . . yes, like making telephone calls she couldn't face making herself. I think this must have been what confused me because when he said, all quiet and respectful, 'I'm afraid I have to inform you that the *padrone* has had a fatal accident,' I couldn't think who he was alluding to or what on earth he meant. If it had been Lorenzo, surely, and if he were indeed dead, then it would be Elvira herself who would be telling me this; or otherwise, if she had not yet been informed, the police. Old Marini just didn't come into it. So I kept asking obtusely, *Chi?* And, *Come?* And, *Scusi*, do you mind repeating that? My attention not so much on the conversation as the receiver, where I had just noticed, encrusted on the holes of the mouthpiece, fascinating little half-moons of spittle that Elvira had always warned me to look out for but which until then I had never believed existed. She had even told me how to get rid of them: 'Spirit and toothbrush, Giulietta *cara*, spirit and toothbrush. And mind you do it yourself: with hidden dirt no maid is to be trusted.'

The implication being that no Englishwoman was to be trusted either when it came to housework, me least of all. No, it took many seconds, perhaps a whole minute or more, for Marini's message to get through to me and when it did I found myself still mesmerized by the crescents of spittle, so that instead of taking in the details as I was meant to, I just went on scratching at these wretched formations with my nail, trying to dislodge them before using the telephone again on my own account.

Which I did immediately I had hung up. Not to impart the news to anyone else – I doubt I would have been capable of that, and who could I have told it to anyway? Franny? My father? – but to check on its veracity.

I rang Elvira at her flat on the floor above ours and got Marini again. His presence there at such an hour brought the truth home to me but stung me as well. On the huge weal of the major hurt it was this tiny scratch of coldness that I felt the most: why hadn't Elvira come down to tell me herself, or sent Nicolò?

'Is it true?' I screamed into the mouthpiece, probably clearing the holes by soundwaves, like the dentist, since I never noticed the phenomenon afterwards that I remember: it was something attached to just that night. 'Is it Lorenzo? Is he really dead? Tell me, for goodness sake. Tell me what's happened?'

Then, scarcely waiting for a reply, I rushed into Bice's little room, dragged her out of bed and told her to stay with Marco no matter what, and bounded up the two flights of stairs that lead to my mother-in-law's apartment on the top of the building.

I almost forgave her when I saw her for her cowardice or thoughtlessness or lack of trust or whichever it was that had prevented her from breaking the news to me in person. She was in such a state. She looked like a waxwork – no life in her at all except for little pearls of sweat that stuck out on her forehead like the tips of hatpins. And even cheeses have that, and certain stones.

My entry – eyes staring, nightdress flapping – acted on her like those clamps you see applied to the dying in television serials about hospitals. Her frame kind of shuddered and jumped, and then kicked back into functioning mode. She rose unsteadily to her feet from the sofa where she had been lying and came towards me and took me in her arms, laying her cold damp forehead against mine. 'Giulietta,' she whispered. '*Piccola mia*. Oh, why did this thing have to happen? Oh why, why, why?'

'It's true, then? He's dead? Lorenzo is dead?' I still had some kind of residual difficulty in believing the fact. A hope, perhaps it was, or a thread of arrogance: me, young, rich, happy, strong – surely there was some mistake, surely life wouldn't dare to pull such a trick on me?

My repetition of the dread word *morto* – such a knell to it in Italian – seemed to cause Elvira to crumple entirely and

3

only the swiftness of Nicolò, shooting out to catch her from behind the sofa where he had been standing with Marini, saved her from falling. Both brothers were always attuned to their mother's needs, though in most cases Lorenzo chose deliberately to ignore them. 'True?' She moaned. 'Oh yes, it's true all right. Even if the *carabinieri* say . . . that the body . . . Oh, the body, the body . . .'

And there, understandably from her point of view but intolerably from mine, she dissolved into sobs and it fell to Marini again to inform me of the full horror of what had happened. No car accident, as I had thus far sort of sketched in my mind for want of other material to go on. Or not, at any rate, the type of car accident I had sketched. Lorenzo had been, yes, at the wheel of a car – a van, to be exact, a Fiat van belonging to the firm – but the vehicle had not crashed or swerved off the road, it had exploded. Killing him on the instant, that went without saying, but otherwise doing very little damage apart from tearing up a metre or two of the tarmac and blazing the leaves off a small tree that grew by the roadside. A hibiscus: I don't know why I remember this, but I do, nor why the police should have mentioned it to Marini or he to me, but he did.

My behaviour was, I now realize, probably already under scrutiny. Whether by Marini or some other member of the household makes no difference and I prefer not to know, but I think it must have been Marini as he was the only person so far, apart from Elvira, to have spoken on the phone to the police. 'Watch her reactions,' the *carabinieri* would have advised: delinquency, in their handbook, nearly always begins at home. 'Watch the widow's reactions and apprise us of them later.' (Alas, I am well up in their lexicon, too.) But I didn't realize at the time, nor would it have made any difference if I had done: my thoughts, words, actions

4

were quite ungovernable. Like a panicking animal whose brain can contain only one idea at a time, and that obsessive, I began blundering round the room asking questions, the answers to which I seemed unable to do anything with except repeat, repeat, repeat in the hope that the words – which were surely familiar? – would eventually begin to mean something.

'They what? They think it was dynamite? Who thinks it was dynamite? The *carabinieri*? What does Lorenzo have to do with the *carabinieri*? Oh, I see, they were called in. Called in where? Where did it happen? On the road to Rignano Flaminio?' (That held me up a while: what on *earth* was Lorenzo doing, in the middle of the night, driving a vanload of dynamite on the road to Rignano Flaminio? And where the hell was Rignano Flaminio anyway?)

The replies to simple place questions like the last were for some reason quicker in coming than most of the others. Rignano Flaminio, I was smoothly informed by Marini, was a village just north of Rome on the via Flaminia.

'The via Flaminia? But that's nowhere near the construction site they're working on now, is it?'

A delayed no, this time from Elvira.

'Then why go there? And why at night? And why in a vehicle carrying explosives? Was there a new project Lorenzo hadn't told me about? Something he preferred to do himself, without consulting anyone else in the firm? Something that involved . . . I don't know . . . blasting or something?'

Elvira turned towards Marini with a beseeching look. Whether it meant, Say that it could be true, or simply, Help me out of this, was impossible to say.

Marini looked down at his long little fingernail kept for ear-cleaning, evidently reluctant to speak.

'They seem to think it was a bomb,' he said at length.

'Of course it was a bomb, if it exploded,' Elvira said impatiently. 'What difference does that make?'

He inserted the nail between neck and collar and began running it to and fro along the gap. 'Explosives explode, Donna Elvira, but not all explosives are bombs. The definition of a bomb, I think . . . I mean what makes it a bomb rather than just a . . . not a bomb, is . . . Well, in part it's the way you use it, the way you go about setting it off, and in part it's the compression. You see . . .' He cast around for some object to illustrate whatever it was he was trying to explain and, after some hesitation, picked on a walnut. There was a whole bowl of them – leftovers from Christmas at Montelupo. 'Now, imagine . . .'

Elvira put her hands over her ears and interrupted him with a cry. 'For God's sake, Marini! Where on earth is your head? We don't want a science lesson. Just say: could it have been dynamite for blasting, or couldn't it?'

Marini flushed and dropped the walnut, and then began chasing it furtively around the floor with his foot. 'No, Donna Elvira, it couldn't have been dynamite for blasting. It wasn't, no. Not according to what the *carabinieri* said. And then there's the question of the register. Any material we use – and we haven't used any for years, not since the motorway contract – it has to go down on the register. Ours and the supplier's. There's a tight check on these things. It's not like . . .' His eyes cast around again and came to rest on Elvira's birthday azaleas, a present from Lorenzo, 'Flowers.'

Elvira looked as if she might be about to fall again, but didn't. 'No,' she said, swallowing, 'it's not like flowers.'

I was still groping. I had followed the exchange in all its detail, but the meanings went on eluding me. All I could do was mechanically repeat my questions. 'What *was* he *doing* with it then? With this bomb or whatever it was? What *was* Lorenzo doing?'

There was a long silence at this point, then an enquiry, this time from Elvira, so soft I could barely hear it, and so strange I could hardly understand it when I did. 'You what?' I finally managed to counter. 'You *what*? You thought *I* might be able to give the answer to that one? *Me*? What in the world made you think that? The *carabinieri* did?' (So, mysteriously, we were back to the *carabinieri* again.) 'They want to hear it from me direct, do they? Why? I see.' (I saw nothing yet, only the smoke from the cigarette that, in my blundering, I had somehow managed to acquire and light.) 'When do they want to question me? Now? No, I don't mind, why should I? You think I ought to speak to who first? To Avvocato Russo? No, I don't mind that either. Whatever you think best. The only thing is that I've left Marco downstairs alone with Bice, and I'd feel happier if I went and . . . OK, fine, I'll do that, thanks. No, I won't use the telephone, I wouldn't have used it anyway.'

On my way downstairs, as if they had needed only this for their ingress – a tiny patch of quiet – the answers I had so far received filed into my head and assembled there in slightly better order. Lorenzo had died in an explosion, the nature and reasons of which were totally unknown to me. Because of his left-wing views and all those dreadful arguments they had always had together, mother and son, reactionary and rebel, Elvira was convinced he had blown himself up, carting the stuff around for some terrorist organization. Likewise Marini, likewise, you could bet on it, the police. Elvira was also – not convinced but let us say suspicious that I was somehow mixed up in the business, too. She had loved me out of duty, turning on me the jet of her maternal affection like a fireman would a hydrant on a blaze – automatically, from good training: but she had never liked me, we were too different, and never really trusted me either, for the same reason. Her last piece of advice – to refrain from using the telephone, which I suppose, with her absurd respect for police efficiency she thought might already be bugged – summed up her attitude very neatly, being both a declaration of loyalty and a covert reminder that, *sotto, sotto,* she believed I was guilty as sin.

I wonder if I have ever felt as lonely as I felt at that moment, standing there on the no man's land of the stone staircase, barefoot, in my nightie, feeling the news I had just learnt drip through into my consciousness: plop and ripple, plop and ripple, item after item, implication after implication? I wonder if I ever shall again? Come what may, it seems unlikely. I doubt even the antechamber of death, when I get to it, will be so stark. Lorenzo gone for ever, in a way which I already sensed would become crueller and crueller and more and more final, the more I learnt about it; his family, never close, now ready to distance themselves even further from me, should this be expedient; my son too young to be of any help, my father in all senses too far away. My friends – well, who could drag friends into a mess like this? The only person at hand to talk to, an ageing lawyer, not necessarily nor even probably on my side. And lastly the police, the *carabinieri*, whirling in like vultures literally any minute now, with anything but friendly intentions in my regard.

No, it was a bleak moment indeed, rendered even bleaker for me by a plague of niggling little thoughts that chose this of all times to surface, such as, Who did the flat belong to now? Whose name was it in? If Elvira's, would she want it back? OK, Montelupo was mine outright, but I couldn't very well live at Montelupo, could I, not when Marco started school? Or could I? And talking of schools, what school should I send him to, now that there was no Lorenzo to consult on the matter? The one he had chosen or the one I myself preferred? The clamour of my bourgeois soul, Lorenzo would have called it, and how right he would have been, and how I longed to hear him say it.

Of what I did in, say, the next half-hour or so, before the lawyer arrived, I have little or no recollection. Vaguely I remember dressing – and I hope I remember rightly, as Avvocato Russo is the most disgusting old lecher, and I would have hated to give him gratification on this score. He calls women he fancies 'pullets': a pretty little pullet, a nice plump pullet. Which of itself is enough to damn him in my eyes. Still more vaguely I remember lugging Marco upstairs, fast asleep, and trying to explain the reason for the transfer to Bice as we went, but she was in such a panic all she could do was splutter, '*L'ingeniere*,' – which is what she called Lorenzo – 'oooh, *poveretto!*' and burst into cascades of giggles.

Did I perhaps have to defend her to Elvira on this account? Try to explain what shock reaction was, and how an unsophisticated country girl of barely nineteen could hardly be expected to control it? Very likely, I was always having to defend Bice to my mother-in-law, one of Elvira's favourite ways of getting at me being through this particular channel. 'That girl!' (A term wide enough to cover both of us.) 'Never laces up his shoes properly, never makes him rest in the afternoons, never allows him to digest before his bathe, never dresses him up nicely when there are visitors. Why you don't correct her, Giulietta, I cannot imagine. I suppose you think it's undemocratic.'

And was this, too, when Nicolò and I had that curious moment of closeness, when we clung to one another with such despair that for an instant I could almost feel his pain bleeding into mine and vice versa? Or was that later, between the talk with Russo and the arrival of the police? Or was it later still, when Elvira was nobbled with

Mogadon and the house, just for a brief space before the telephone began again, settled into something like its old quiet night-time self: ticking clocks, dozing cats, and the smell of acacias wafting through the balcony windows? I used to love the smell but now I'm not so sure.

The conversation with Avvocato Russo I do remember of course, but not as well as I ought, and almost certainly not the bits that I ought. Even at the time I had trouble remembering those.

We were left rigorously alone together: Elvira in a plea that struck me almost too fervent on my behalf had insisted on that. I don't think I had acquired yet that shiftiness that goes with innocence when innocence is not credited, but I was fast on the way to it, and the Avvocato if anything speeded my progress.

No counsel, I think, would have been better than the counsel he gave me. No counsel, or else a few little pills of it, fast-working, easy to swallow. 'Keep off politics altogether,' for example. 'Do not allow yourself to be drawn out on this subject. Say you knew nothing of your husband's opinions and have none of your own, full stop and *basta*.' Or else, 'Answer all questions promptly but volunteer no information on your own account. Truthfulness should not be confused with babbling.' This too would have come in useful. Or else a simple reminder that the police interview was informal, that no charge had yet been made and no crime proven.

Instead, in typical forensic fashion, or Italian forensic anyway, he began trying to explain to me with astounding verbosity the judicial side of things – both as they stood and as they would stand if I was so incompetent as to muff my answers with the police. Hence I came away from the encounter with my head reeling with unfamiliar words – most of them, both in Italian and the English I so desperately tried to translate them into, beginning with an 'i'. *Istruttoria, indagine, inchiesta*, inquest, inquiry, indictment, *indizi, imputazione, interrogazione, incriminazione*. (Only 'inquisition' was missing, but that would add itself later.) That and a sense of fragility with respect to authority that I had never known before except in theory.

'The watchdogs of the bourgeoisie' we had used to call the police, Lorenzo and I, in the days of the student uprisings. And then bark at them: woof, woof! and make slurping sounds. Easy to mock from behind a protective barrier of caste such as ours.

And now the barrier was down and the dogs were coming for me. Not vultures, no, that was a careless metaphor, vultures attend to corpses, but a pack of ruddy great mastiffs, jaws wide, baying for my blood.

Although in fact, when it came to it, the *carabinieri* were surprisingly restrained, almost gentle. At least in their face-to-face dealings with me: they had less restraint later when it came to searching the flat, and none at all at Montelupo, where they wrenched up a whole patch of flooring – it was loose and must have caught their eye on that account – knocked a hole in the wall where I had once wanted a hatch put in and then had had blocked up again when it proved so draughty, and even uprooted my precious plot of rhubarb. Mistaking it no doubt for a cannabis plantation: terrorists, drug addicts – the equation was quickly made in the official mind. I dread to think what they would have done had they come across the syringe we used for injecting woodworm fluid into the beams, but luckily Ubaldo found it first and threw it away. Bless Ubaldo.

Anyway, with me, that night, the *carubba*, as Nicolò called them, had their kid gloves on. The family being what it was and the doubts on all fronts being what they were, they must have deemed this kind of approach more

11

prudent. 'Terrorist's Widow Confesses' made one kind of reading in the headlines, 'Widow of Accidental Bomb Victim Grilled for Hours by Police' made another, 'Widow of Lorenzo Gherardi, head of the well-known building firm, who recently lost his life in a cowardly Neofascist assassination plot, etc., etc.,' made yet another.

How curious it is, looking back on things, that this third possibility took so long to surface in my mind. Shock is hardly a sufficient explanation, although I honestly can't think of another. Had it been anyone else involved in the disaster, any of our friends for example, it would have been the first thing I would have thought of, the Neofascists – *i Fasci* (again a term I borrow from Nicolò). They were doing things like this all the time, all over the country: committing crimes that the Left would never have been foolish enough or evil enough – or even organized enough for that matter – to commit, and then leaving a huge red signature with arrows underneath it pointing in just that direction. 'We did it – the Marxists, the commies. Come and get us!' So why not in this case also? Nothing easier, nothing cheaper, nothing more efficient at the price, just slip a bundle of sticks of dynamite into one of the vehicles belonging to that bolshie young Roman industrialist Gherardi or whatever his name was, and sit back and wait for the fireworks. Might get a bricklayer, might get the *capomastro*, might, if you were lucky and did your homework right, get the boss himself – in any case, it'd make a nice stink.

As I said, the design was so clear and so familiar. And so fresh, too: there'd been an episode only a couple of weeks back – a kidnapping in Milan involving some factory manager or other whose photograph had appeared in the papers, the drawing of a red star, of all lunatic things, hung round his neck. Lorenzo and I had discussed it for hours – the typical fascist jargon of the message: Bite and run! Strike one to teach a hundred! And yet I don't think it was until the *carabinieri* themselves suggested it, or implied it by one of their questions, that I suddenly woke up to this likelihood of the Neofascist attack. No, stronger than a likelihood, this certainty.

The higher-ranking officer – a colonel, I think he was – was immediately alert to my change of stance. Until then, if I'd been thinking at all, it was still in terms of an accident, a straightforward accident. For some absurd reason this presented itself in my mind as the only alternative to Lorenzo's guilt. Which I refused even to contemplate, knowing as I did, utterly and absolutely and no matter what anyone else might think they knew to the contrary, that he was innocent. That he had never, not only been a terrorist but met a terrorist, flirted for a second with the ideology, thought a terrorist thought or performed a terrorist action. Be it only, as was hinted in this case, the transport of dicey material.

'Then you admit it's possible your husband *was* involved in some kind of terrorist activity, Signora?' the officer put in nimbly, stretching out his logic like a trip-wire.

I saw Avvocato Russo widen his piggy eyes in warning. No, I said, that wasn't what I said at all. I said I thought he might have been the *target* of terrorists. Were the people in the bank in Piazza Fontana involved in terrorist activities, simply because they were killed by a terrorist bomb?

'Ah, but that is different. That was a left-wing attack, the killers were anarchists, and the victims were there by chance.'

'The case against the anarchists isn't proven yet,' I objected. 'In fact it looks as if they might soon be let off.' I was about to add, 'And I hope they are,' but stopped when I caught Russo's eye again.

'Aha.' The Colonel looked grave and heaved a profes-sional-sounding sigh. 'So you share your husband's left-wing political opinions then, Signora Gherardi? I'm not sure we were clear on this point. Or were we?'

I ignored Russo's oglings, which, had they been noticed by any of the *carabinieri*, I think would have landed me in gaol faster than a confession. 'Yes, I do,' I admitted. 'Naturally I do.' And then proceeded, in an outburst that surprised all of us, myself included, to tell him why. Starting with the careless days in Cambridge, when Lorenzo and I had met and fallen in love, and thought of nothing but ourselves and the cars we would buy and the journeys we would make and the clothes we would wear and the night-clubs we would visit and so forth, through to our gradual awakening to the seriousness of life and our duty towards others less lucky than ourselves. Our conversion, I suppose it was, our road to Damascus. I had never put it in words before, except once, to Franny, sort of, and she had looked embarrassed and said it sounded half-baked. And I'm afraid she was right, it did. Especially in Italian.

As I neared the moment when we had made the jump from morals to politics and taken up membership of the Communist Party, Russo, until then I think rendered lit-erally speechless by my initiative, suddenly bustled forward and began making noises. Splutterings to begin with, then a sort of cover-fire of protests. It was late, he said, I was tired and under great stress; there was still the taxing business of the recognition of the deceased to be performed. If ques-tioning of his client were to continue it should continue next morning, or better still after the funeral. There was nothing to be gained from listening to the unbalanced and totally irrelevant outpourings of a mere relative, as he was sure the *carabinieri* themselves would be the first to admit.

The Colonel's expression implied otherwise, but at this

point my stomach, which had been misbehaving ever since I'd lit the cigarette, went into cramps, causing me to blanch and buckle and to earn my first anything like approving glance from the Avvocato.

Very well, the Colonel conceded, after I had been moved to the sofa and given a tot of brandy by I know not who, that went down me like fire. That would do for tonight. But I was to hold myself in readiness for further questioning. Once the *istruttoria* (oh Lord, here it came, one of those threatening 'i' words) had been opened the magistrate in charge would almost certainly want to speak to me in person. And at length.

As he and his colleagues prepared to take their leave I could see them looking around at the furnishings with a novel kind of disgust. All this on a plate, and the idiots went and voted Communist! What was Italy coming to?

In quite another key it was more or less what I was thinking myself. What was Italy coming to, when it had people in it capable of murdering in cold blood a person like Lorenzo? For the first time since he brought me here I had the perception that I was on foreign soil, and some daft little nationalist stowaway inside me, that I never knew I carried, whimpered for England.

CHAPTER TWO

The passage through those days seems, in retrospect, to have been like the descent of a spiral staircase into hell. Each tortuous step lower than the former, when you could have sworn while standing on it that the former was the lowest you could ever reach.

The breaking of the news. The seeping in of the news. The horrible, horrible adjustment to the seeping in of the news, so that what a few minutes earlier would have been uncontainable, unbearable, is in fact contained and borne: grief bloating the heart, rupturing it, taking away all its sinew.

Then the morgue, with Elvira insisting on seeing the body herself, so that, although I didn't see it – couldn't, didn't want to, didn't even think it would serve a purpose – I was forced just the same to see it through her eyes afterwards.

The mortuary police tried so hard to dissuade her, to convince her to allow some other, more distant member of the family to perform the duty in her place. But she, who never normally questions things like that coming from people in authority, suddenly got all dramatic and suspicious and said – no, screamed – that the police were hiding things from us, and that they were worse than the Colonels in Greece, and she would never believe Lorenzo was dead until she saw him with her very own eyes. And on and on until one of the officials raised his shoulders and nodded and said, *Vabbè*, in a defeated voice, If that was what she really wanted . . . And then led her away, and brought her back again with that ghastly imprint on her eyes that transferred itself in a flash to mine, and that was almost worse than seeing.

If I had thought this was the nadir, however, I was wrong because then came the funeral. The funeral, with the placards and the red banners and the clenched fists punching the air, and the skirmishes and the caterwauling, and the police cordons and the photographers clambering over one another to get a picture of the coffin. I would have been proud for Lorenzo if I had thought any of this belonged to him, whether as tribute or just a plain salute to a fallen comrade, but none of it did. Even the speeches, when they came, had nothing personal about them; they were mere hectorings, and the speakers professional agitators cashing in on the occasion. All the workers from the firm, in fact, stayed silent, limiting their expressions of sympathy to a huge white wreath of carnations (white, not red, I especially noticed the colour) and a handshake afterwards that, in several cases, was almost impossible to exchange, the press of strangers being so thick.

It was a nightmare day from start to finish. From the morning, when I awoke to the sound of Marco's chirpy, happy voice informing everyone, 'My papi is dead, my papi is dead.' (How long before he realized what it meant? Already, from the repetition, you could tell he had picked up something jarring in the phrase.) From that heartrending little bugle call, on and on to the never-ending evening with its never-ending round of visitors: family, friends, friends of family, families of friends – each person's face, with a very few exceptions, covered with a veil of embarrassment of

17

varying thickness, and behind it, a question of varying thrust. Poor girl, does she realize? Funny girl, did she know? Foolish girl, why didn't she stop him? Shady girl, was she in it, too?

Elvira was magnificent throughout: loyal, serene, to all appearances unshakeable, not a hint of the conflict that must have been tearing at her mind. That's part of her trouble really, she is so very gifted, so powerful, so energetic, that she is only able to stretch herself to full span in a crisis. Perhaps she ought to have been a firewoman or something, rushing from one blaze to another, always on emergency call. And had she been one, perhaps everyone else in her entourage, me included, would have been more comfortable, as we wouldn't have had to function as mops for all her surplus emotions and whatnots.

That evening, in flashes, I knew I loved her, even though she would never love me back; knew also that I was jealous of her, of her beauty, and the hold she'd had over Lorenzo, and that I resented the way she managed to conquer others by soft means that for me would never work: tears, reproaches, innuendoes, smiles. But the knowledge was quickly gone – swept away by the usual waves of exasperation she managed to stir up in me.

Next morning, with no occasion for steam letting, she was back to her pressurized self. A spring aching for release. I could see her casting around for any outlet I could provide her with, and, most of them proving too dangerous, finally settling on what she called my 'riccio' way of dealing with my grief. A riccio being a hedgehog. 'I can't get at you,' she lamented, though we both of us knew it was better for her not to try. 'I can't reach you, curled up tight like you are. If all of us do that – just roll ourselves into a ball, turning our backs on the others – how will we ever get over this tragedy? Mourning is something people ought to do together, Giulietta. Look at the Greeks. Look at the Sicilians.'

I didn't want to look at the Greeks or the Sicilians, I wanted to be respected as an individual, however quirky, and left to my own devices. The last thing I needed was to be drawn into a contest to establish whose grief was larger and whose claim to grief stronger (which is where I suspected Elvira was trying to draw me). Yet at the same time, the moment she'd said it I couldn't help, inside myself, doing just this: getting all uptight and muttering to myself in an injured fashion that I *was* Lorenzo's *wife*, for goodness sake, and that surely I had the right to mourn for him as I saw fit?

And then thinking, Yes, but what if I had lost Marco instead of Lorenzo? Surely a mother's grief is more unbearable still? And feeling ashamed in Elvira's regard. And then cross, because I had been piloted yet again, and going off to the courts without asking her to accompany me. Which was all she'd wanted really in the first place: just something to gnaw on to stop her gnawing at herself. And then, naturally, feeling the shame coming back. Oh hell.

All this was a pity, because I could have done with some support on that morning in particular, since it turned out to be the moment I really did reach the lowest step. Or so it seemed to me then, with the sounding equipment I had then.

It was the day of my first interview with the Pubblico Ministero, the magistrate who, as the *carabinieri* had warned, was now responsible for the conduct of the case – or inquiry or inquest or whatever it was that *istruttoria* corresponded to. (Which, like cuts of meat, was probably nothing, the whole system of division being different in the first place.) Avvocato Russo referred to him, rather intimidatingly for an English person like myself, as the PM. In turn I tried to cut the office down to size by suggesting

19

'coroner', but Russo was horrified. '*MOLTO più impor-tante*,' he said with a huffing sort of emphasis on the *molto*. '*MOLTO più importante*.'

From the room into which I was ushered – all on my own: for some perplexing reason, so long as I was considered innocent I was not allowed to bring a lawyer with me – you wouldn't have thought so. That the man inside could be important, I mean. It was a cubicle more than a room. A low, smoke-filled cubicle of a dark-yellow colour, dark-brown lino on the floor and dark once-upon-a-time white on the ceiling: a place for curing haddock, or so it went through my mind.

Occupying virtually all the space was a desk, of the kind you see in really posh schools where appearances are scorned. A dreadful old crate of a desk – stained, scarred, branded by countless cigarette stubs. This, a coat stand, a waste basket, a filing cabinet and a trio of Formica chairs, completed the furnishings. If furnishings you could call them: they didn't really furnish, they just filled. The desk top, also Formica, also brown, was bare, save for a metal ashtray, a large notepad and a clumsy old telephone. The waste basket looked as if was empty. There were no personal touches, almost no touches of occupancy whatso-ever. Just the smoke and the occupant himself, a man of – I had difficulty guessing – forty, I would say; thirty-eight, forty, forty-two, that sort of range, who was speaking into the telephone as I entered.

This gave me a chance to look at him, because after-wards, with the scrutiny going so pressingly the other way, I hardly could have managed. I'd have been like a novice tennis player, up against Panatta. My first impression was that he was bloodless, that by his sojourn in the room he had literally, like a haddock, smoked himself dry. Most people have red or pink about their faces somewhere; his had not a spot of either. The eyes were brown on a bluish field, the mouth and skin ochre-coloured with, again, metallic bluish patches where the beard glinted through. The hair and eyebrows and the rims of the eyes were corvine. Most faces, too, have fatty bits, round areas, even if it is only the curve of a cheek or the bulge of a nostril, but this one was entirely angular, entirely spare.

Like a perplexing modern painting you are afraid to rubbish, I felt neutral towards it to begin with, disposed to think it either beautiful or ugly or neither, pending a later reading, but the moment it turned fully towards me I came down unhesitatingly in favour of ugly. *Hässlich*, I thought in my O-level German – ugly and hateful together.

The first words he spoke to me, after he had finished in an insultingly leisurely fashion his telephone conversation, were to ask whether I wanted tea or coffee or anything to drink before we started, and instead of relaxing me they threw me into panic. Probably, it struck me a little while later, because he reminded me of the picture in one of my childhood books of Pluto, King of the Underworld, and to accept his hospitality was therefore to succumb. Or maybe I was muddling him with Bluebeard – blue jaw, blue beard – who was in another book in the same series. Anyway I jumped like a frog and said No with unwarranted loudness, and I saw the long black-rimmed eyes narrow with suspicion at my nervousness, and we got off to a bad start.

'How old are you, Signora Gherardi?'

I couldn't see the point of that question, but still. I told him I was twenty-seven. He did not appear to believe it, although whether he thought the figure too high or too low was unclear. Maybe neither and he just wanted to show me from the very start how deep was his mistrust.

'Passport,' he said curtly, stretching his hand towards me

across the desk and tapping on the lino impatiently with nicotined fingers.

After he had consulted it he gave a grudging nod, but did not hand it back. Making me even more nervous, because Russo had listed this, the detention of my passport, as one of the worst things that could presently happen and (his exact words) a *pessimo segnale*, a very bad sign indeed.

'Juliet is Giulietta in Italian, is that not so?'

I nodded and waited for the mention of Romeo that I could sense was about to come – as it generally did, Italians in the main not shunning the commonplace, in fact diving straight for it as often as not. But all I got was an ironic twist of the mouth, just stopping short of a sneer, to show me the connection had been made and found inappropriate.

'And More is Più. Giulietta Più.'

For a second I thought he was about to make a joke or use my Christian name or something, and panicked again, it seemed so weird in the circumstances, but no, thankfully he stuck to the distance and the 'Signora' and the third-person singular. Side-stepping the matter of Lorenzo's death entirely – no mention, no offer of sympathy, nothing – he began asking a series of routine questions on the lines of the first: place of birth, name of school, number of close living relatives, addresses of same, place and circumstances of meeting with Lorenzo, date of marriage, number of children, length of time spent in Italy. He took no notes of my replies and to all appearances scant notice either, but the questions, which you'd have thought would have been over pretty quickly, my family being just me and Father and my schooling lamentably short, went on and on. Standard of education reached? Mother's maiden name? Date of mother's death? Cause of mother's death? Father's profession? And more I can't remember. I got the impression his distaste for my person was so great that he could hardly bring himself to draw any nearer than this – to the framework of my life, as it were, and no further. Like someone who has found a myxy rabbit, and can only prod at it from afar, with a stick.

I had expected the opposite – the light in the face and rake through the brain approach – and dreaded it, too, but after a while of the stick treatment I began to think it might be preferable.

When at last it came, however, it was not. The switch was rapid and to my mind slightly forced, as if learnt from a manual. Torquemada Tips, How to Rattle a Witness, Judge Jeffreys Reveals All. Something of that kind.

There was a brief silence, then in a voice suddenly charged with anger – no, worse, it was chillier than anger, it was distaste again, contempt – he leant forward across the desk and said, straight into my face, so that I caught a whiff of the tobaccoey breath, noxious at this time of the morning, 'Why do you think you are here?'

I shook my head and said I didn't know. It sounded vapid. What I meant really was that I didn't know which way to answer the question.

'Hasn't your lawyer explained your position to you? You do have a lawyer, I presume?'

'I . . . No . . . Yes . . . No, I mean so far I have been helped by the family lawyer, by my mother-in-law's lawyer, but . . .'

'But?'

But nothing. Every word I said only seemed to deliver me tighter into his clutches. Information would be my pomegranate. I shrugged and remained silent.

He shrugged, too, as if in mockery. 'Your position,' he said in a flat voice, looking into my eyes without somehow meeting them – just scanning, 'is potentially very grave. I don't know how far you realize this, but I think it is only fair for me to warn you. You are in a very delicate position indeed. Terrorism, even for flanking members who do little else apart from carry messages and darn holes in balaclavas, is a crime that carries severe punishment in this country. We are talking, Signora Giulietta More-in-Gherardi, in terms of thirty, forty years. Mull this over in your mind for a few moments and then try again to answer my question: why do you think you are here?'

The mention of darning balaclavas was fortunate. It whipped me beyond self-consciousness into something approaching rage. Also the way in which he used my name, as if it were an insult. 'I don't know what I think any more,' I said, 'but I know what I thought before I came in here: I thought I was going to meet someone who would help me find my husband's murderers. That's what I thought. That's what I hoped.'

'Really?' The tone was one of gelid surprise. 'Murderers, eh? I assumed from my reading of the police report that you tended to favour the thesis of the accident. Is the report incorrect, or has something happened in the interval to make you change your mind?'

The question was full of traps, I was sure, but I didn't dare stop to look for them or he would have seen my hesitation and construed it God knows how. 'I changed it that same night,' I said. 'While I was talking to the *carabinieri*. They asked me something about telephone calls and whether we'd had any strange ones lately, or messages or anything, or seen any strange people hanging around outside the house, and it suddenly struck me . . .'

'That you had?'

'No. It suddenly struck me that Lorenzo had been murdered. That they – the *carabinieri* – thought it, too. Thought it possible anyway.'

'And you immediately thought it certain? From a

24

shadowy possibility you jumped immediately to full certainty? Snick, like that?' And he snapped his fingers with a loud brittle sound – even they were dry.

I thought of the funeral. What was he trying to insinuate? He must have seen the photographs in the papers. 'I'm not the only one to have done that.'

'You are the only one, Signora, at present, whose motivations concern me. How the crowd arrives at a particular conclusion is something I can learn from your great dramatist Shakespeare. If I'm interested, which in this case I'm not. What I want to learn from you is how *you* arrived there.'

'The same way, of course. By putting two and two together. It's so obvious. Look where we're living, look what's happening every day around us. Look at the violence of the Right, look at the attacks on students, look at Reggio Calabria, and that cache of arms that was found the other day in Milan.' I remembered something Lorenzo had recently said about a survey that had been done in Lombardy, but I hoped I wouldn't be asked by what organization, as I couldn't remember. 'Do you know how many incidents of fascist violence have been recorded over the past two years? Four hundred, four hundred separate incidents. That's one every two days. More.'

Fool, but now I'd said it. 'Toh! You are very well informed. Let me turn the question round then. *Since* you are so very well informed on these matters, how is it that the question of a possible political motive behind your husband's death did not occur to you sooner?'

There he had me. I was still bewildered about this myself and could only make an on-the-spot guess. 'I don't know. I suppose . . . because we are ordinary people; because things like that don't happen to ordinary people. At least . . . yes, they do, but when they do, you don't sort of . . . think they can.'

It was a very weak answer, and yet for some reason I could see it pleased him. For the first time he reached for the notepad and scribbled something – very brief – on the opening page. 'You thought this. Hmm, I see. Yet it didn't take you long to change your mind and plump for political murder?'

'No.' I sensed I was being cornered, perhaps already had been, but saw nowhere else to go. 'It didn't take long.'

'Then it is lucky you possess this faculty of rapid change of your opinions, because I think you're going to need it again. Very shortly.'

I waited. I wouldn't give him the satisfaction of asking why.

'It is like this, Signora Gherardi: I have not yet received the official forensic report, but it is the opinion of the field investigators – who, believe it or not, are quite experienced in these things – that your husband's van was at a standstill when the explosion took place and that he himself was holding the bomb in his lap. It would take a very cunning murderer to get his victim to do that, don't you think – actually cradle a primed bomb in his lap? Not to mention making a getaway before the thing went off. And it would make for a very funny kind of accident, too. Or not?'

I tried to absorb this news without showing how much it shocked me. Henceforth I realized news would probably always come like that: brutally, slantingly, in the form of a trap. Translatable or not, the meaning of 'istruttoria' was coming home to me. I screwed up my eyes, trying to blot out the image of Elvira's face at the morgue. What happened to a body when a bomb exploded in its lap? That happened. And what happened to the person who had loved the body? Ah, that I would discover on my own account. 'But you say it's not official,' I finally managed to stammer.

26

He said something, incomprehensible to me, about it being *ufficioso* but not *ufficiale*. I had never understood the difference between the two forms. However it gave me time to think.

A little. 'He could have found it,' I said, as soon as the thought had solidified. 'Lorenzo could have found the bomb in the van, and been holding it for that reason. In order to get rid of it. You know – throw it away.'

My questioner tilted his head back. I thought I read boredom in the gesture and it almost made me want to cry – that he should dare to be bored, by Lorenzo's death, my pain, everything – but luckily I didn't and went on being angry instead. 'The bomb was equipped with a radio-controlled detonator,' he said.

No, it wasn't boredom, he was watching me far too closely. 'What does that mean?'

'It means it had a device rather like a remote-control switch for television, if you are familiar with those gadgets. A beam that you set to a certain frequency and a button that you press to spark off the detonator and detonate the bomb. This device was found among the wreckage, badly charred, almost melted, but identifiable all the same. The investigators think it likely it was at the centre of the explosion or very nearly. Do you need me to spell out the conclusion this points to? I hardly think so.'

As a matter of fact I would have appreciated help, my thoughts were in such a tangle; but I was too proud to say so. 'Likely is not certain. You said so yourself just now.'

'No, likely is likely. But judges are accustomed to working with likelihoods: we would hardly be necessary if proofs were always certain.'

Out of the tangle a strand emerged. An end – something to pull on. 'And this remote-control device, is it unique, is it

27

just for that bomb, and is it the only thing that can set it off?'

This earned me a first glance of true curiosity. It was harsher than the others, which was saying quite something, but it heralded a slight change of attitude. I thought for a second this might be because the magistrate, or judge or whatever his office was, had realized for the first time I was sincere; but I don't think it was that, not yet, it was more the realization that, truth-teller or liar, I might pose something of an obstacle.

'In theory, no,' he said. 'In theory any kindred device set at the same frequency can do the task just as well. Any radio signal even. Even a chance one, if you happen to be so unlucky. But again in practice I hold it so unlikely as to be hardly worth looking into. Ockham was a countryman of yours, no? You are familiar with his razor?'

Thank God I was, enough anyway not to make an utter fool of myself by looking surprised. Although in a way I was surprised. Indignant is perhaps closer. 'Yes, I know what you mean all right,' I said. 'But how can a maxim like that possibly hold good with criminals? Isn't that the whole point, with criminals – that they are trying all the time to put people on the wrong track? Muddle the clues? Shift the blame on to others?'

He looked amused – just very faintly. If he had said anything about my having read too many detective novels I think I might have spat at him. But he didn't. Which in a way was a shame. 'Meaning?'

Quick, think. 'Meaning that whoever it was who let the bomb off threw the radio device deliberately into the explosion area afterwards to make it seem it was Lorenzo who had used it. Or . . .' I immediately saw the weakness of this: they'd have had to throw it at the exact moment of the explosion, and how could they have got that close? 'Or

28

planted it there deliberately in the first place. Packed it up with the bomb, so that it would look as if it was the mechanism that had been used to set the bomb off, when in fact . . .'

'When in fact it was a second device, operated by wily right-wing terrorists who, one, knew exactly where your husband was going and at what time, two, could pinpoint in advance the exact point along the road at which he intended to stop so as to hide themselves there in readiness, and three, knew that when he stopped he was going to obligingly discover the bomb and place it in his lap, and then sit there waiting for them to blow him up. Is that what you were going to say?'

I was silent, fighting hard against tears, which were threatening stronger and stronger. No one ever before had treated me with such a sustained barrage of scorn. I was sure there was an explanation that accorded with my own theory, and that it was in some way connected with these radio thingamajigs, which – who could say – maybe could be used at great distances, or from moving vehicles or – oh, I don't know, in a fashion, anyway, that had enabled Lorenzo's unknown enemies to commit this terrible deed against him and escape the blame. But I realized that if I voiced my opinion – any opinion – without working it out properly beforehand, it would go the way of the other – straight into the rubbish bin. I needed to know more about the technical side of things first, and I needed to think, think, think.

Fortunately the PM said no more about the explosion, evidently considering the matter closed – at least for the time being. Instead he began asking me about journeys. Dates and journeys. Mine and Lorenzo's. How often had we travelled to places together, how often apart, for how long, on what days? Had either of us been to Milan at the beginning of February this year, or in late November the year before? What about Trento in the summer? And Lake Garda? And the year before that, 1970, what journeys had we made then?

I am hopeless about dates; I asked if I could consult my diary and let him know the details later. Lorenzo and I had been to masses of places, I explained (slightly huffily: I resented the insinuation – unvoiced but nevertheless clear – that Lorenzo had concealed some of his movements from me). His work took him all over the country. And now my son was older and I was freer, I often went along with my husband, too – just for the ride, just to be together. Sometimes I would go into the office or wherever it was he had the appointment and sit there and read a book until he had finished, and sometimes I would just stay outside in the car alone and listen to tapes. It depended. But without the diary . . .

No, he broke in sternly, no diary. I was to tell him all I could remember now. The *carabinieri* would take care of the diary, they would be bound to find it during their search.

Search? I stiffened. What search?

The search of my apartment, of course. He had signed an order authorizing Colonello Vitali to conduct a search of my apartment that very morning. The villa in the country, too.

Instinctively a protest squeaked out of me but I smothered it before it became words. Obviously a search, if it is to yield any fruits, must be done without warning. I couldn't quarrel with that. Indeed it was strange, when I came to think of it, that it hadn't been carried out earlier: since the night of the explosion, if I'd really wanted to, I could have hidden all sorts of things, done away with all sort of things. How lucky it was after all that Elvira hadn't come with me today; she would be at home to take care of things and make sure Marco didn't have to watch while a herd of policemen rummaged through his father's possessions.

'You are worrying about your child?' How the hell did he know and what the hell did he care? 'You needn't. The *carabinieri* are trained and reliable people, they will cause as little disturbance as possible. However . . .'

Another trap, I could sense it. He was going to offer me the chance to go home, now that I knew about the search, and see whether I took advantage of it. If I did it was because I was nervous and had things to hide. 'Yes?'

'However, if you think you would rather be there yourself . . .'

I shook my head, and stole a quick look to see if he seemed disappointed I had avoided the snare. But he didn't, he looked critical, as if he was mentally chalking up 'bad mother' beside my name.

'Today's is only a preliminary meeting anyway,' he went on. 'I have established no line of inquiry yet, drawn up no particular schedule. I merely wanted to see you, find out if we could work together.'

What a vile suggestion. Unfortunately my upbringing tricked me into responding automatically, 'And can we?' before I could check myself. It sounded weak, pathetic, and opened me wide up to his reply.

'I had hoped so,' he said. 'It rather depends on you. If you see reason and decide to tell me frankly all you know about your husband's terrorist activities, yes. However little that may be, however much. If you continue to maintain your position of pretending to believe he was innocent, then, no. It's a question of choice.'

'I can tell you about my husband's activities,' I said. 'I can tell you all about them as frankly as you wish. But I can't tell you about his terrorist activities because there aren't any, there weren't any, there never were.'

He looked sad now as well as bored. I hoped he was, and on valid personal grounds: I hoped his wife had left him for the plumber, and his fillings had dropped out and he couldn't pay his mortgage and . . . oh, the works. 'I see,' he said. 'If that's the way it is, then . . .' Click. He made a clamping gesture with his hands that I didn't understand.

'Then what?' I asked.

He sighed. 'Then we stay together, we sit together, we talk together, we argue together for as long as it takes me to make up my mind about the truth of what happened that night on the road to Rignano Flaminio, but we do not work together. No working relationship, you understand?'

I understood enough. That it was a declaration of war, more or less. But what did it matter? Better war than collaboration with such an enemy. 'That *is* the way it is,' I said, looking him straight in the eye.

'Very well.' And without any change of expression whatsoever he returned to the dates and the journeys. Using his earlier method of questioning, flat, rapid, impersonal, but somehow, now that I had experienced both methods, even worse than the other, even more inimical. It was like being tapped on the temple by a giant woodpecker – tukka tukka tukka tukka tukka. The notepad this time was in full use.

I don't know how long the questioning continued in this manner, nor how well I stood up to it from a defensive point of view. The tempo was such it didn't really allow you to monitor things like that, and I suppose that was its whole point. I had nothing to conceal, and by the same token nothing to reveal, but all the same I felt violated by the time it stopped – plundered, deprived of some essential part of me, though what it was I couldn't say. Dignity, I suppose. Self-regard.

This, I now understood, was the non-working relationship, the pattern of things to come.

In silence my interrogator scribbled a few more lines on his pad, then turned it round and presented it to me for signing. I did so straightaway; it never occurred to me I might have powers of refusal.

'Thank you, Signora Gherardi.' The voice contained no feeling any more, no qualities, not even disdain, not even contempt – those had been concessions, little windows on to his mind that meanwhile he had thought better to shutter. 'That will be all for the time being. Any questions before you leave?'

I strove for the same tone, but I was so bruised inside it didn't really work; you could sort of hear the swelling. Lorenzo would have detected immediately what he called my Pagliacci quaver. (Oh Lorenzo, Lorenzo. Which was worse: to go on holding him in my head all the time, or to let go and have him coming and going, each entry a gash?) 'Yes, one question. May I leave Rome at all in the interval, or do I have to stay put?'

I had suddenly decided that I must go to Montelupo, now that the *carabinieri* had been there, and explain things in person to Ubaldo and Cesira. They had been at the funeral but, discreet as they were, they hadn't made it through the crush, only sent out messages with their eyes, appalled, from a distance. I was ashamed I hadn't rung them, but perhaps Elvira had done it for me, it was the sort of thing she never overlooked.

'Of course. You can go wherever you like. Even back to England if you like. As long as you are here punctually for our next meeting. Which will be,' he took out a smaller notebook from his pocket and flicked through it; the pages were almost black with appointments, 'on Friday morning at the same time.'

I was about to ask after my passport but he forestalled me, sliding it towards me across the desktop. The finger that slid it, however, remained firmly pressed on the cover. 'One thing, Signora Gherardi, before you go. This is a personal piece of advice and I hope you will not interpret it as interference, but if I were you I would engage an independent lawyer, one of your own choosing. It is always wise for a person to have a lawyer of their own.'

I couldn't think what he meant by this, nor what he meant to achieve, unless it be to weaken my ties with the family and isolate me still further. Of the whole interview, which had contained a fair selection, it was perhaps the most disquieting moment of all. I waited till the finger lifted, grabbed my passport and fled.

CHAPTER THREE

Marini came to fetch me from the courts. I would have preferred a taxi but there was none in sight. And anyway, there he was – obliging, deferential, handy. Oily as a fish liver.

'Signora Giulietta.' Deep bow, almost insult-level. 'The Signora Contessa sent me.'

Lorenzo had hated this way of referring to his mother, always interrupting whoever it was who used it to explain that titles of nobility had been done away with in Italy since the proclamation of the constitution in 1948. I would never have his patience, or his grit. 'That was very kind of her. And of you.'

'Been quite a morning,' he went on as he steered me by the elbow through the chaos of the parking sector. 'One way and another.'

I didn't want to learn about the search from him. Nor did I want him to learn anything, about anything, from me. I pleaded a headache – which after all the drilling was only too real – and got into the back of the car. Lorenzo always said this was wrong and that you should get into the front, but I honestly couldn't face Marini's nearness, nor his look of disapproval should I flout the conventions.

I got one anyway, I don't know why. Perhaps because I

wasn't wearing black. I would never wear black, it was the fascist colour. Just as I would never wear a leather overcoat or crop my hair or own a Doberman pinscher.

When the car drew up in front of the doorway I could see Elvira on the lookout on the balcony above. She came downstairs to meet me, a glass of Fernet Branca in her hand. Her favourite offering: prize and punishment in the same bottle. But she was buoyant again on the tide of crisis and had forgiven me my earlier meanness. 'How did it go, *piccola*? What was he like, this Carosi? Tell me everything, I want to know everything.'

We had been given the PM's name the evening before – a courtesy information from one of Elvira's beaux in the Ministry of Justice – but it had slipped my mind and for a moment I hardly knew who she meant. It seemed far too normal to fit the fiend.

'You tell me first,' I said. 'What have they done? Where's Marco?'

Elvira, bless her in this instance, and curse me for not blessing her more often, had seen to everything. Marco, she informed me, was in the kitchen having his lunch, and then he and Bice and the housekeeper's son were off to the cinema to see *Bambi*. The *carabinieri* had gone, taking with them, as far as she could tell, nothing except a wad of papers and the old air pistol Lorenzo had used to shoot beer cans with when he was at school. The flat had been set more or less to rights, but the books would take time – there were so many of them and all had been torn out of the shelves and riffled through.

'What did they think they'd find in books?'

Elvira looked at me thankfully. Whenever I said anything innocent-sounding she rewarded me with this look. 'What did they think they'd find anywhere? Oh Giulietta.' Her eyes suddenly filled with tears, 'I . . . I . . .'

'You?' I prompted cautiously, I didn't really know if I wanted her to continue.

Maybe she read my misgivings. 'Nothing,' she said, tilting back her head so that the tears went in again. 'Nothing, it was nothing. Tell me about Carosi. How it went off.'

'He's a swine,' I said. 'A fascist pig.'

The thankful look vanished, to be replaced by something much more familiar. 'Then don't tell me,' she said. 'Honestly, Giulietta, you can't go around just sticking labels on people. I had a long talk on the phone this morning with Russo's partner, Avvocato Luini – I'm not sure he isn't better than Russo, better informed. And he told me that we have been lucky with the PM, that the man is known to be sound and independent, that he's not tied to any particular party and he'll give us a fair hearing.'

'He's tied to the Right, though. He's a swine, Elvira, I guarantee you. He's got it all made up in his mind. He's not going to listen to what I say, not unless it fits in with what he wants me to say. He's made up his mind Lorenzo was a terrorist, and nothing, nothing is going to move him from that.' I was on the point of saying he thought I was one, too, but checked myself: Elvira didn't need any extra nudging in that direction.

She heaved a sigh with tremors in it. 'Oh dear,' she said generically. For a second our eyes met on exactly the same frequency (like the radio beams the PM had told me about?) and we looked at one another in naked despair: two incompatible strangers marooned together on an island, dependent on one another and aghast at being so. Then she turned away. 'And what did you say?' she asked into her Fernet.

I told her, more or less – as much as I could remember. But by the time I had reached the business of the journeys I

37

could tell she had stopped listening. Her mind, too, like Carosi's or whatever he was called, was made up about Lorenzo's guilt and she was trying so hard to come to terms with it that she just couldn't afford any back-tracking, any deviation. So I stopped telling. 'Your father rang again,' she said, to fill the silence. She got on surprisingly well with my father, and vice versa. 'You'd better ring him back. There's just time before lunch; we shan't eat until Nicolò is here.' A pause for change of register. 'I shan't eat at all.'

'I shall,' I said in a belligerent, contradictory fashion. Which was quite unnecessary of me.

'Yes, well.'

'And I shall ring my father this evening, from Montelupo. I'm driving there this afternoon with Marco and Bice, the moment they get back from their film.'

This on the other hand was necessary, although I suppose I could have put it in a gentler fashion. The longing for Montelupo had become a kind of physical ache inside me. Fear, yes, of a place where Lorenzo and I had been so happy; reluctance, too, almost shame, to enter it in my new state; but a longing far stronger than either.

I knew only too well the response my decision would evoke from Elvira. Montelupo? Now of all times? I must be mad. Only this morning she had tried to explain to me the importance of sticking together, and here I was, proposing to go and shut myself away in that freezing old barn on the hilltop. It was a ridiculous idea: I would be cold, I would be lonely, I would be at the mercy of the journalists, should any of them discover my whereabouts, and have no one to fend them off. *She* would be lonely. I oughtn't to deprive her of the child at this moment. (True, only Marco bored her stiff in doses exceeding five minutes per day.) It was quite wrong of me to put this added burden on her shoulders: she would be worrying about me constantly.

38

What would I do in the evenings, she would like to know? Sit around and mope and play cards with the nursemaid? That couldn't be healthy. What was that? Say it again. Come *with* me? *She* come with me? To the country? In March? With all the things that needed doing here in Rome and all the people she had to see? *Insomma!* How could I make such a suggestion? How could I be so . . . so different, so strange, so (she groped for a stronger insult) . . . Anglo-Saxon?

By the time Nicolò arrived the objections had all been listed and relisted and smoothed away and ruffled up again, and we were sitting there at the lunch table, his two leading ladies, in one of our typical cease-fire silences. Uncomfortable always, but now, with grief pulling us close and stripping us raw of all protection, pretty nigh unbearable.

I could almost see his heart shrink at the sight of us. What a heavy mantle to fall on his shoulders at the age of barely nineteen: the nominal chieftainship of this lacerated house. He kissed his mother first, and then came round to me – slightly more spring in his step, so that all three of us could see it was the less onerous task.

'We are losing Giulietta this afternoon,' Elvira told him, in a high-pitched, announcer's voice, as he sat down. 'She has got it into her head that she must go to Montelupo. She needs to be' – she made it sound an outlandish requirement and selfish beyond belief – 'alone.'

'Uhuh.' Nicolò nodded and delved into his soup.

There was silence, while we both watched him. It was nice somehow to see hunger, appetite – a face so like Lorenzo's, involved in the business of living.

'When Nonna Vinca died,' Elvira went on after a few moments (Vinca, or Vincenza, was her mother, who I never met), 'your cousin Simone came over from America for two and a half months, just to keep Serena and myself company. I have never forgotten that gesture.'

Nicolò continued with the soup. 'He lost his grant,' he said when he'd finished. 'Simone forfeited his grant. I bet he didn't forget it either.'

Elvira turned round and signalled to Corrado, her new Venetian manservant, to bring in the next course. Poor man, he looked miserable: you could tell he was longing for the trial period to be over so that he could give in his notice and wing it back to the quiet of the lagoon. 'That's not the point,' she said. 'It's the distance, the worry, the not knowing what the other person is doing. Giulietta, whether she realizes it or not, has had the most terrible shock. And shock can lead people to do any number of unpredictable things. You can call me neurotic, an emotional blackmailer, anything you like, but I shan't be peaceful in my mind – not for one single instant – knowing that she is caged up there in that great barn of a place, alone, grieving, at the mercy of the press, without someone reliable to take care of her.'

Nicolò looked up suddenly from his plate and across at me. 'I'll go,' he said.

Elvira's voice changed. From plangent to crisp. 'No you will not,' she said quickly.

'Why not?'

'Why not?' (A question repeated, I had learnt from my morning's exercise with the PM, was a bid for time. Elvira was in difficulty: she still had grave doubts about my innocence – that was clearly the root of the trouble – but she couldn't express them, she could only cordon me off with regard to her second son.)

'Because I need you here, that's why. I'd have thought you'd know that without my having to tell you. I need you,' she inhaled and her magnificent breasts swelled like spinnakers, 'desperately.'

40

'Uhuh.'

Nicolò went back to his food. He sounded detached, but I could tell somehow he wasn't. Lorenzo's death was going to have a lot of consequences for him as well, not least a show-down with his mother at some point in the proceedings, if he wasn't to go under completely. Younger sons in Italy can get things in a roundabout way and remain integral – it is almost expected that that is the way they should be: velvety, vulpine, a touch elliptic in their dealings. But elder sons, such as he had now become, had to conduct the power struggle head on. It was an unwritten tenet of family law. I think he knew this, and dreaded having to put it into practice.

It was up to me to smooth things over in the interval. 'I'll invite Franny to come with me, Elvira,' I said. 'If you like. If it will make you any easier.'

I meant to be conciliatory, but the meal was as illogical as the Mad Hatter's tea party. Elvira rose to her feet and let out a wail. 'Your friend Frances? Your English friend? The one that is married to that little jumped up cockatoo of a polo player? Giulietta *mia*, don't do that, I beg of you. Please don't, don't do anything of the kind. Not on my account. There is no need . . .'

No need for what? Obscurely her worry angered me. Hadn't she just said she didn't want me to go alone? Well, then, I would ring up Franny and we would go together. It was that simple, I couldn't see what all the fuss was about.

And yet in a sort of way I could.

'Oh really!' Elvira sat down again abruptly, in high huff. 'What world *are* you living in, I sometimes wonder? You really are too extraordinary. One tries . . . one does one's best, and then, time after time, one meets with . . .'

'With what? What's wrong? What have I said wrong?'

She tossed her head with such force that her chignon

41

came unanchored and fell sideways, over her shoulder. 'Nothing. Go ahead. Telephone this Frances friend of yours by all means, if that is what you want. Pay no attention to me: after all, who am I? Just your mother-in-law. And what am I trying to do? Just protect you, that's all.'

Protect me? From *Franny*? I looked at Nicolò for guidance or interpretation, but he just shrugged.

'Go on,' Elvira urged, making shooing gestures with her hands so that her rings clattered. Was it possible she had already lost weight? 'Telephone. Invite your friend Frances, I'm sure she'll just jump at the offer.'

So that was what it was. I thought as much. Elvira was afraid Franny would let me down; chicken out on account of all the fuss in the papers and stuff. How little she understood – about either of us. Franny and I had been friends long before we came to Italy, and had stayed friends always, even though we lived such different lives and were married to such different people. We never went out in a foursome of course, that would have been unthinkable (although I have a sort of feeling that we did think it once, with grim results, and succeeded in forgetting about it). Nor did we live close enough to see each other without hassle – Lorenzo and I being in Parioli in the north part of the city and Franny living right out in EUR at its extreme southern tip. But nevertheless over the past – what did it come to? Six years of school, plus three of flitting, plus seven of marriage: that made sixteen. Over the past sixteen years we had never lost touch, never grown away from one another. And never, never let each other down in time of need.

I said as much to Elvira, getting quite worked up about it. Again, I don't know why, but for some reason the issue seemed to me to have national undertones. Franny was English like myself, and *because* she was English – not so much because she was my friend but because she was

42

English – she would somehow be deaf to all the gossip, immune to all the doubts. Steadfastness was an especially English virtue, it suddenly struck me, friendship between women likewise. Italian females, schooled to geishadom, just didn't understand.

However, as so often when I grew emotional, Elvira went the other way, towards dryness and scepticism. '*Sarà*,' she said lightly, pinning up her tumbled hair. No doubt I was right. There is hardly a more dubitative formula in the whole Italian language.

Sadly I wasn't right, I was dead, dead wrong. When we set off late that afternoon for Montelupo there were just the three of us – myself, Bice and Marco. Marco in a *piano* mood on account of *Bambi*, which, with the profile of the father figure in high relief, had not been well chosen. There was death, too, I had forgotten. He kept on asking questions. Where had Bambi's mother gone? Would she come back? Why was snow so cold? Could he have a gun to shoot things with? When? How big?

I was scarcely in a frame of mind to give good answers – admitted that there were any. Franny hadn't refused to come exactly, but – oh Christ – she had been so strange and shifty on the phone, I would almost have preferred it if she had done. 'Not on your nelly, you rabid old red,' she ought to have said. Or, 'You're in the shit OK, for God's sake don't drag me in it, too.' Answers like this I could have dealt with. But, no, she just dithered. 'It's not a very good moment; maybe later; Carlo has got this thing on at the club, you see, and I promised . . .'

I knew it wasn't really her, but the dreaded Carlo. Lorenzo had always disliked him. He said the man was a money snob, and only tolerated the friendship between Franny and myself because we were so rich, and because he liked saying, 'My wife is staying in the country with the Gherardis,' to all his polo cronies; and also because it suited him to rid himself of Franny for the summer while he nipped down to Positano in his third-hand Porsche to act the playboy. Staying with the Gherardis – with this stink of dynamite and terrorism in the air, more kudos now in staying with the Borgias.

All the same, the rebuff cut deep. There would be other slights, I could see that now. Other slights from other unexpected quarters. Indeed the social consequences of Lorenzo's death would probably, like the soundwaves of the explosion itself, continue to journey through the atmosphere on their own account for many months, maybe years, now and again, like this one, reverberating with a sting. But Franny's denial was the first and worst, and it was a sobering reflection to realize I would have done better to listen to Elvira after all.

Ah well. I had wanted solitude, hadn't I, and now I'd got it. Both my passengers fell fast asleep in the back of the car the moment we left the motorway, and as I drove on in the gathering darkness through the cleft of the Nera valley I again experienced the isolation I had felt that first night on the staircase. Only this time it was pure solitude, not loneliness. The outward journey to Montelupo had always cheered me, just as the return had always done the opposite. So much so that I had come to associate the geographical altitude with a corresponding lifting or drooping of the spirits: Nera Montoro, my mood already well above sea-level, the climb to Narni and another rise, San Gemini and I could feel the cares dropping away like ballast from a balloon, and then the last sharp uphill stretch to Montelupo itself with each bend bringing me a little notch higher until at the start of the drive itself I felt practically ready to fly.

No flying tonight, but nevertheless the old hoist mechanism worked to some extent because with the passing of the kilometres I began to feel calmer inside, and my stomach, which ever since the breaking of the news had felt as if it had been scoured with acid, began to settle. I thought of food, without interest but without repulsion. I thought of the fires which Cesira would have lit; our beds with the 'priest' inside – a wooden frame for raising the covers, with a warming pan at its centre. (Why 'priest'? I don't know, nobody did, but everyone laughed when they said it, as if the origin lay in some forgotten local smut.) I thought of waking – OK, alone, in pain, but in my favourite bed where Lorenzo had bullied me with heroic perseverance into my very first orgasm; where we had had 'flu' together for an entire fortnight and completed in desperation a 10,000-piece jigsaw; where we had fought and read and talked and – oh, if I really named everything we had done in it, the list would have more items than the puzzle. The sight of the beams – solid, beautiful, honey-coloured – which were the first thing that met the eye; unless you were lying prone, in which case it would be the similarly mellow surface of old, polished and repolished terracotta tiles. The noise of one lone moped, one tractor, in place of the Roman traffic roar. The smell of fires again – fresh, morning fires – as Cesira prepared breakfast for Marco in the kitchen. Toast and jam – a foreign meal to her: 'Why isn't the poor little *potto* having salami and tomatoes and fried-up pasta? That'd keep him going through the morning. No substance in this fancy stuff, whatever you city folk think.'

I was edging minimally away from my unhappiness, or so it felt, but I had reckoned without the pathos of arrival. Ubaldo in particular. Ubaldo without Lorenzo. I could hardly, now I came to think of it, imagine the two of them divided. Their friendship had been instantaneous, almost magical; its closeness and improbability had earned them the name in the village of the fiancés – *i fidanzati*. What did they have in common, the rich young city intellectual and the sixty-year-old ex-miner, now retired and living off a barely decorous pension? Politics? Yes, in the strict party sense, but not only that. Local power politics as well. A love of gossip, a love of the countryside, a passion for walking, for driving off in the land brake on urgent business that took them half the day and five coffee stops; a yen for inspecting drains, for hunting truffles, for picking mushrooms. All this, and yet it still wasn't enough to explain the delight each drew, across the divide of age and class and experience, from the other's company. I suppose the nub of the matter – where reasons and explanations neither fitted nor belonged – was that they loved one another, full stop.

The dogs ran out to meet the car as we crossed the gateway – three absurd little sausagey poms: anything larger Ubaldo would have considered dangerous – so I knew, even before I saw the lights in the windows, that he and Cesira were there, waiting.

They came out to greet us, and in the semi-darkness Ubaldo let out a kind of bellow and moved towards me with lowered head, as if charging. He reminded me of an old wounded bison.

'Giulietta!' he cried as he staggered forward. I had always begged him to do so, but this was the first time he used my name without the 'Signora' tacked on to the front of it. 'How is it possible? Him first, before me? What's this old man good for? What am I going to do? Eh? Eh?'

I held out my arms. Again, out of respect I don't think there had ever been more contact between us than a handshake – twice yearly, if that. But now we embraced with the practice of decades.

Ever since the brief outburst with Nicolò I had tried to dominate my grief, sit on top of it as it were, especially in the presence of Marco. And mostly I had managed; although each close friend of Lorenzo's, as I met them for the first time after the tragedy, set up a different problem, touched different wounds in me that needed individual staunching. The funeral had called for this intervention over and over. But this encounter was different; the wounds just too many and too messy to deal with. So we stood there clasping each other and sobbing, with no control at all – at first just the two of us, and then Cesira, who threw herself across us like a rugby player, making three, and then Marco, who sort of wormed his way into the knot at leg-level, dragging behind him Bice who otherwise would have been left out. It was real collective mourning for you, but not perhaps of the kind Elvira would have approved.

When we separated I felt lighter, I don't know why. As if the tears had been lead or mercury or something and I had literally shed weight in getting rid of them. Marco was still howling like a banshee, and I was suddenly prompted to tickle him, so that he began laughing as well.

I'm not sure we didn't all laugh after that, I know Bice did because she had another fit of the giggles and earned herself a sound slap from Cesira, who had no time for psychology. I think I did myself, too, on account of Bice, but then I entered the doorway and saw the state the floor was in and stopped.

Cesira misinterpreted my look. 'We were just cleaning up,' she explained hurriedly. 'We've been at it all day, they made such a mess. Didn't they, Baldo?' And she nudged Ubaldo slightly forward. 'There was no stopping them.'

I had thought up on the way various different preambles to ease us over the embarrassment of the search and all it implied, but now I scrapped them as unnecessary, even pernicious. 'They think he's guilty, you see,' I said, looking full face at each in turn. Two old-fashioned faces – no, timeless faces, fashionless faces, but nevertheless very typical of the region; faces you could find in Giotto, Perugino, in an altarpiece of Gentile da Fabriano, always in the background. 'They think he was on his way to blow something up and blew himself up instead.'

Both husband and wife drew breath through rounded mouths. 'Oooh!' But this was just courtesy: they knew perfectly well – the whole village most likely knew perfectly well and talked of nothing else.

However it wasn't the news itself that was important, it was the confidence. Which I decided might as well be total, having got this far. 'They think I may be involved, too. That's why . . . all this thoroughness.' And I gestured towards the remnants of chalky rubble.

Cesira tossed back in scorn her red-grey hair, that she wore still in a Veronica Lake curtain, loose on one side, and Ubaldo gave another of his bison bellows. 'Guilty!' he let out in a huge voice, causing Marco to start and then look at him in fascination. 'I'll give them guilty!' He shook his fist in the air: I don't think I'd ever seen that done before, not spontaneously, not off the stage. 'Rats! Insects! Reptiles! *Screanzati!* If he's guilty – if Lorenzo's guilty – I'll . . . I'll . . . I'll . . . tear up my party card, I'll become a monk, I'll lay myself down on the railway and let the trains run over me. Guilty! Him a terrorist? When he wouldn't even let me spray the greenflies, he had such a heart.'

'I know.' How simple he made it sound, and how simple it all suddenly became.

'They got him, that's what. Those blackshirts, those fascists, they got him. Though there'll be trouble proving it, I dare say. Those fellows that were here – they couldn't nail a criminal to save their lives.'

48

Cesira nodded. She only ever contradicted Ubaldo about planting. On every other subject his word was gospel.

I nodded, too. 'I know,' I said again. What a relief it was – at last – to be in the company of people who believed utterly and absolutely in mine and Lorenzo's innocence. Even my father over the telephone had had just tiny reserves on this point (I expect he'd caught them from Elvira), which translated into a smudge of awkwardness between us. But Ubaldo and Cesira were stauncher than any relative; doubts of that kind just never entered their heads.

'Terrorists are fascists. The Left has never gone in for that stuff, that . . .' Ubaldo spat the word out in fury, 'muck. There aren't any red terrorists, they're black, the lot of them.'

'I know, I know, I know.'

'And your husband, Giulietta, was a good man, a man to be proud of.'

I knew that, too. Lorenzo, you might say, was my measuring stick of goodness, my touchstone; I scarcely had one before I met him.

Ubaldo put his head in his calloused miner's hands and shook it from side to side. 'This is not a just country,' he said slowly and with great solemnity. 'A country where a thing like that happens to a man like that – no, it is not a just country.'

The echo of my own thoughts on the night of the tragedy was so faithful, and I was so surprised to hear it coming from this source, that all I could do was to stare at him and murmur yet another, I know. But this time Ubaldo seemed to hear me differently, with new ears; or as if the words themselves were new and he had just this moment grasped their meaning.

We looked at one another, and I saw his forehead expand and the lines on it become less marked, as if some kindly spirit had applied a compress. Anguish easing; sorrow making way for something else. Then the moment passed, and without any further talk on the matter we trooped outside again, all of us, and began the routine task of unloading the car.

It wasn't good to be back here, but it was less bad than any other place I could imagine being.

CHAPTER FOUR

One of the things I had decided during the drive to Montelupo – almost the only thing really of any clarity – was that I would spend as much time as I could there thinking.

There were so many things I needed to think about. Lorenzo's last evening. The last time I spoke to him, the last time I saw him. Any eventual clues, hints, indications that some person or group of people was keeping watch on him, had him so to speak in their sights. The *carabinieri* were right about this: there must be some pointer somewhere if only I could distinguish it, if only I could remember.

Then – or possibly before that – I must think about the things that could help me to think, better than I would otherwise think without them. Make a list, for example, of the people I ought to speak to and the questions I ought to ask. A bomb expert, maybe a radio expert as well, in order to be better prepared for my next interview with the PM. That was the first requirement. Though how the dickens I would find either of these fairly highly specialized technicians . . . Ask Piero, that was it. Piero first on the list, then the two experts, then – who else? Lorenzo's secretary, Giovanna, to find out about his last day, or days: the people he'd met, the calls he'd received, any unusual things he'd done or asked her to do for him. Who, for instance, had been the last person to see him before he set off on his errand? Find this out, too, for God's sake, and quickly. Find out what they talked about, whether he mentioned, either to them or anyone else, his coming trip to Rignano Flaminio. If so, did he give reasons? Then still more practical things: the van – how exactly did he get it? When, at what time? Did he ask someone to prepare it for him, fill it with petrol and stuff? Did he have to sign for it? Who besides himself knew that he was going to make use of it? Where was it parked that day? Who had access to it? Yes, the van was crucial, all these things were crucial. And crucial, too, was the fact that the police and the PM would never bother to investigate any of them. Not properly. Why should they, when they'd already caught their terrorist? No, this kind of detective work was up to me, and me alone.

And yet, and yet . . . intentions are one thing but the contents of a head are not so easily marshalled. I had decided all right to get these things straight in my mind, but when it actually came to it I found my thoughts drifting with the woolliness and stubbornness of so many sheep, not forwards but backwards.

A long and quite unnecessary way backwards, to the time of my first meeting with Lorenzo and our first months together, before marriage. Hence every time I lay on the bed, or went for a walk alone, or curled myself up in the armchair in front of the fire while Marco was watching telly, and said to myself, Now, the list, start making the list, instead of doing that I would find myself back in the Whim or somewhere, or Jesus Lane, or the banks of the Cam – nineteen years old and plunged headlong into my first comprehensive affair: head plus heart plus body.

Only the heart was a bit tardy in following the other two. I remember sitting over crumpets with Franny, discussing

52

what I should do, how far I should yield to Lorenzo's pressure, that was already nudging me southward, towards his home and a meeting with his family. She was involved with a Frenchman at the time – a Breton, I think he was; very jealous, very bossy – and in no position to criticize what to other friends might seem a surrender, a giving in to a superior force of will.

'Do you love him then?'

'I don't know. Do you love yours?'

'Jeannot? No, but that's different. Jeannot would never ask me to marry him, he's far too prudish, he wants a virgin.'

'This one is serious, Franny. I wish he hadn't asked me, and then I wouldn't be in such a spot.'

'See the family first, and then just . . . see.'

'See Naples and die.'

'Is he from Naples? God!'

'No, you nut, he's from Rome. Oh, please, Franny, be serious. Tell me what you think of him; tell me what you'd do if you were me.'

'You really want to know? Well, I think he's . . .' Long pause, so she really is considering the matter. 'Too intense, that's what. I'd be scared to get involved.'

'*Intense?*'

'Yeah, there's something – a bit heavy about him, you know what I mean.'

No I didn't. There was nothing in Lorenzo's make-up, so far as I could see, that smacked of weight or weightiness. In fact, if anything, I would have said then he was frivolous – a flitter, a skater on life's surface. Funny things seemed to interest him (although I suppose this judgement was naïve and I should have looked at the *quality* of the interest, not the object it was directed at – skaters after all can be dead committed): materials, jewellery, shoes, the cut of clothes.

Shoes in particular: he would spend ages in front of shoe-shop windows – assessing, praising, decrying, trying to get me to see the, to me, persistently invisible entity of what he called the 'line'. Car racing, he liked that, too. James Bond novels. Seafood. Riding macs, made-to-measure shirts. And screwing with me in every possible place and time and position.

This last taste, memorywise, was so painful that each time I came up against it I shied off, grazed to bleeding point. Which made it difficult to follow any memory at all, since all inevitably had led, sooner or later, to this conclusion. Desire had been the cement, the glue of our relationship, and possibly the building blocks as well. *His* desire – so constant, so powerful, so overriding as to suffice for both of us: I didn't want him, not then, but I wanted him to want me, needed to see his need; and from it – by inference, like a doctor reading a thermometer and concluding from its markings that the patient is still alive – to know that I was female, beautiful, attractive, arousing, possessed of all the qualities I most wanted to have and most doubted that were mine.

Two rudderless ninnies, that is what we were, steered by Lorenzo's hormones and little else. Even Marco I remember carrying as a sort of patent: Look, someone needs me so badly as to put me in this shape, and I need them so badly as to put up with it.

Pampered ninnies, too: we had everything, on a huge gold-rimmed plate. I had no idea that Lorenzo's family was so rich, nor that my father (who had no idea either, or he might have reconsidered) would make me such a large marriage settlement. We had a flat, ready and waiting; we furnished it like wanton squirrels. We bought Montelupo, we furnished that, too. We bought a sports car, an Alfa Romeo, that drank petrol like an open plughole. We had friends by the dozen, from all walks of life, but we could hardly understand the poorer ones when they declined to come on trips and things – how could they be such spoilsports? – and finished up, like rich people do, with the rich ones, who could keep our pace. We ate out a lot. We danced the twist in night-clubs. We invited friends to Montelupo and dabbled in Hameau-like rusticity. Our interests flagging, we went in for spiritism and really thin watches.

I can see us at it now – the spiritism lark. Curiously it is one of the very few pictures I carry in my head of the period, and certainly not for its beauty. There are eight or ten of us, sitting out on the terrace on a warm Roman evening, our bodies converging over the iron table top as we strive to keep our forefingers on the bucking, upturned glass. (Some of our feet probably converging as well, underneath the table, for such are our amusements and such the extent we indulge in them.) The men wear high stiff collars sealed with Paisley ties; the tie knot is tiny, its fashioning a science. The hair above the collar is long and licks Caesar-like round the contours of each bronzed and cologned face; the jackets – discarded – are of ochre gabardine, or maybe navy blue. The females, self included, don't even run to a colour change: one and all we sport blonde-meshed hair, a skimpy black dress, black stiletto shoes and a single rope of pearls. Cor!

Then what happened? To Lorenzo and me, to turn our svelte images virtually overnight into the gypsy raggedness of a Baez and a Che Guevara? Was it during pregnancy that I began reading the book about the school in Barbiana? Or was it later when I was breast-feeding? Or was it Lorenzo who began first, and did I just tag along behind out of habit?

I remember it this way, but Lorenzo, when we once tried

to work it out together, remembered it differently, so I may be wrong. Anyway, I remember it like this, that I was sitting up in bed, reading this strange little booklet that someone – I think it was Rita or Piero or both – insisted I should read, and a passage struck me, and I read it out to Lorenzo, and he said 'Nonsense' and then 'Give it here' and snatched the book away and started reading it himself. First silently and then, when I protested, out loud.

The thesis of the book was simple, and simply set out: it maintained that the dominance of the bourgeois class over the labouring class was engineered and perpetuated by a conspiracy. A conspiracy which my father would have only half jokingly referred to as 'Keeping the Buggers Down', but which to the authors of the book had nothing joke-worthy about it at all. It was a 'sampler' work, nominally concerning only the fortunes of a tiny remote mountain school and its pupils, but in fact pointing an accusatory finger (no, a clenched fist was more like it) at the entire educational system of the Western world.

Only this you realized gradually, and it felt – since the authors themselves kept carefully in the background – that you were discovering these things for yourself. It was like seeing a photographic negative for the first time in your life: black where white was, light where you had come to expect dark. Language – a social invention to enable people to communicate? Maybe at the outset, but in a bourgeois culture such as ours, a network of shibboleths, designed to put people in their place and keep them there. The school curriculum? An e-ducation for pupils, a leading out? No, a re-pression, a ramming them back into their stalls. Exams? Openings, rungs for promotion up the social and economic ladder? Nothing of the kind: closures, crossbars impeding access. All the perks and prizes of the bourgeois system, in fact, nothing but dressing, to give people the comfortable idea of living in an open society, while in reality the levels were sealed off from one another tighter than the sluices of a lock.

I can remember even now the terrible surge of guilt as my Roman Catholic conscience received this information and tried to process it. A tiger cub, watching Mummy do the shopping; a Mafia child, suddenly learning what Dad does for a job. Only I wasn't a cub or a child, and neither was Lorenzo.

'What do you think?' I asked anxiously, hoping to hear him snort and toss the book aside. 'Could it be true? Could things really be like that? A kind of winnowing arrangement – tacit, top-secret, yet connived in by everyone . . .'

'Sssh. *Zitta!*' Lorenzo went on reading out the text. Figures, tables, percentages – the bones behind the flesh of the theory, the proof on which it rested. Instead of following I felt my mind stray back to a childhood game I had used to play with my dolls: the new, pretty ones were me and my friends, and slept in cots and wore the nicest clothes; the old battered ones were thrown into a trunk in their tatters and christened 'the village children'. I had played it without malice, bowing to what I had thought was an inevitable law: among the old dolls indeed were some of my very favourites, but they were uglier, more worn and more unlucky, and therefore the trunk was where they belonged. What if the world was fashioned on these lines: nobs and villagers, the chosen and the rejected; and in the middle a capricious creature like myself (only an entire class, not a person), making the selection on horribly biased criteria and then shutting fast the trunk?

'We need to read more,' Lorenzo said at some point, when the figures got too unwieldy for him as well, and handed me back the book.

I agreed. But what? Where did we start?

Another superfluous question because in fact we had already started. The main batch of recommended names was probably in the book itself, although I'm not sure it carried an index or anything as canonical as that: Marx, Engels, Lenin, Bakunin, Proudhon, Paine, Owen, Marcuse, Mao Tse-tung, and for some reason I was never fully able to grasp, two contemporary British psychologists, Laing and Cooper, and the German idealist philosopher Hegel.

Religiously – and the word is not casual – we made our way through the key texts of all these authors: grateful when the key was of the skeleton variety but unflinching when it was not. Brecht also, in snippets, and any members of the Frankfurt School we could identify and lay our hands on. Walter Benjamin in particular, again on grounds that remained shadowy to me and still do, had the force of a must.

We read at night, in bed, sitting up straight, shoulder to shoulder, something Quakerish in our pose. Sex in abeyance, dressing gowns round our shoulders, hair – at least my hair which has always had an opulent quality about it, at odds with serious social study – tucked firmly away behind the ears. Mostly we read in silence, but I was the less educated of the two and when I ran into difficulties – over the meaning of a word or a sentence, or sometimes an entire paragraph – I would turn to Lorenzo for help.

A system that worked fine to begin with, until I began to notice that the longer the query, the shorter the answer tended to be, and the shorter Lorenzo's patience. At which point I went and bought myself a dictionary instead – a philosophic one – in a vain attempt to avoid friction. In fact my progress only sharpened our tiffs: over Hegel I seem to remember us actually fighting, cuffing each other over the head with pillows.

Nevertheless, in spite of differences we continued to pool

our conclusions at the end of sessions, and this, for me, who was the slower and more painstaking reader, was perhaps the most fruitful time in terms of the knowledge I acquired. The booklet turned out to be right in its every part, and only wrong in limiting its conclusions to education: the world, the Western world, was run, *all* of it, on the lines of a huge conspiracy. Whether consciously or not on the part of the beneficiaries had little importance: exploitation was at the heart of all human dealings. Exploitation of the poor by the rich, of the gullible by the cunning, of the weak by the strong. Exploitation of workpower and resources on every scale, from the smallness of the home, where the fangs of the individual adult male latched on to the veins of his unsuspecting wife and offspring, to the vastness of the continents, where the two arch-villains, North America and Northern Europe, bled into a state of anaemia their weaker neighbours: suck, suck; guzzle, guzzle. Gold, electricity, tobacco, gas, petrol, elbow grease – all down the insatiable twin throats they went.

It was, yes, like discovering some awful, unmentionable family secret. But at the same time it was like joining another, far larger, far friendlier club. A club, moreover, of which your own family had always disapproved, and always told you was a sink of perdition; making membership, when it came, all the more rewarding. The Left, the reds, the Marxists, the communists – the bogeymen, the baby-eaters, the enemies of the state and all the state stood for. This was how the members of the club had been described to us, and this was how we had trustingly (and most ingenuously) assumed them to be. And now we drew near to them, these demons in human form, and discovered that the reverse was true: that they were our friends, not enemies, and that they were victims of the system and not its aggressors.

The man at the paper stall, until yesterday a stranger, suddenly noticed our switch of reading matter and greeted us with ear-to-ear smiles, neglecting his other customers in order to pass us first our copy of *L'Unità*. The sullen-faced waiter at the bar downstairs, also on the basis of the newspaper, I think, which he must have seen sticking out of Lorenzo's pocket, took to winking and calling him '*compagno*'. Vice versa, the picture framer on the corner who had always been obsequious, to me in particular, hoping for patronage, now turned his back on us when we passed his shop and buried his nose firmly in the right-wing daily *Il Secolo*.

In a way it was like being a fragment in the lens of a kaleidoscope after a shake-up. All the pattern of your relationships haywire of a sudden, and everything having to be re-mapped, re-plotted – not only minor allegiances like these with locals and tradespeople and so forth, but major friendships as well. Out went the natties – mostly of their own accord, scandalized by the talk that now crossed the table top in lieu of the Ouija glass. In came the shaggies – *back* in, in some cases. Sergio, another Cambridge inmate, known there as the Red Baron and hitherto shunned by Lorenzo who, on the one occasion our paths had crossed had dismissed him to me with loathing as an '*arcistronzo*' or arch-idiot. Vittorio, a fellow student from earlier days at Rome University, avoided likewise on account of his political 'idiocy', and now sought out and re-embraced as a soul mate. Marta, school companion, rediscovered in the local Communist Party meeting point, the '*sezione*'. Her husband Torquato. Sergio's girlfriend Claudia. These became the kernel of our new group of friends. The only couple from the earlier group to weather the shake-up and remain attached – and very closely at that, in spite of sheering at the last fork and becoming socialists instead of communists – being Piero and Rita. The initiators. Or what Elvira called the troublemakers.

Poor Elvira, rough times for her. Watching the metamorphosis – the flush spreading over her beloved firstborn like the scarlet fever, redder and redder and redder – and knowing she can do nothing to stop it. Discovering in fact, to the contrary, that her every intervention, be it scene or mockery or argument, only serves to speed the process up. Don't for God's sake do that, and Lorenzo straightaway goes and does it. Me, too, though not with quite the same relish. Don't go on marches, and we go on them, savouring for the first intoxicating time the bloodrush as we merge into the throng: this is power, this is benign power, and we are caught up in it and we are, in tiny part, its makers. Don't get involved with those absurd students, and that is precisely what we do. Lorenzo even lends material for the barricades inside the University City and helps set them up. He comes back home one evening out of breath and chuckling: the police have chased him unsuccessfully over the campus yelling, Get the one with the beard! Don't grow a beard – well, too late for Lorenzo but I at least obey that injunction. Don't trouble the rest of the family with your opinions – not the old uncles and people, they would have a fit. Don't talk politics at mealtimes. Don't start catechizing Nicolò, I shall never forgive you. Above all, whatever else you do, don't, I implore you, go and join the Communist Party, anything but that. And, not quite the very next day but within a month or so, we are card-carrying members.

No, it was useless, try as I might to concentrate on all the far more pressing matters that needed investigating, it was here, in this earlier period that could yield nothing but cafard, that I was stuck.

And remained stuck more or less for the whole length of

our stay. Only on the last day, the Wednesday, and then only reluctantly, did my mind let go of the past and begin to move forward again. But sluggishly, without conviction. The famous list that was to have been so helpful grew no longer than its original outline: see Piero, see Giovanna, question both. And then Elvira rang to say Carosi was busy on Friday and had put our appointment forward to tomorrow, and please to come back immediately, so in the end I didn't have time even to perform these two simple tasks but went unprepared again into Pluto's den.

CHAPTER FIVE

'I am not asking you to betray *anybody*.' There was exasperation in Carosi's voice, but I didn't think it wasn't genuine; he was trying to browbeat me into feeling irrational, that was all. 'I already know who your friends are. I don't need you to give me their names or tell me where they live or how far left their political sympathies lie or anything like that. I merely want you – for your own sake, for your own safety I might even say – to think carefully about them, and then tell me if you have ever had occasion to suspect that your husband was meeting any one of them – how shall I say? – with particular frequency, on his own, without your knowledge.'

It sounded more the question of a divorce lawyer. A prurient one at that. And who was being irrational now? If the meetings had taken place without my knowledge . . .

The voice came back expressionless and yet managed to convey rebuke. 'You know perfectly well what I mean, Signora Gherardi. I am looking for a link, a contact. These people are close-knit, wary of infiltration. It's a bit like membership of a club: before they admit a new member they need an old one to sponsor him – someone who knows him well, and has done for some time, and is willing to guarantee he's not an informer. It is this person I am after:

your husband's guarantor, his sponsor.' A wait, with the keen jet eyes trained on me like searchlights. 'Well?'

At one time I had, groundlessly I think, been rather jealous of Marta. Just to begin with, after the rapture of the old school friends' meeting and all the 'Do you remember So-and-so's?' in which I couldn't join. I'd sometimes had the feeling she and Lorenzo got together now and then *à deux*, to natter about old times. Not that there was anything wrong in that. 'No,' I said quickly. I knew Carosi couldn't read my thoughts, but silences were best avoided. 'No.'

'Aha. And that goes for men as well as women?'

Brrh! He gave me the shivers. 'That goes for men and women. Both.'

'I see. I have spoken to your husband's secretary, Signorina . . .'

So at least he was doing some homework. 'Beltrame.'

'Yes, Signorina Beltrame. She says the telephone calls to your husband's office from a certain Sergio were very frequent. That would be your friend Dr Alberici, I imagine?'

That would be the Red Baron all right, the ex-*arcistronzo*. 'Most likely. Dr Alberici is a lawyer, he does arbitration, I think it's called. He and Lorenzo often worked together – when there were disputes and things to be settled on behalf of the firm.'

'They knew each other before, though?'

He *had* been doing his homework while I was away, quite thoroughly. 'Before what?'

'Before Dr Alberici qualified as a lawyer.' The desk had more papers on it today, and Carosi ruffled through them as if in consultation. But my impression was that he had everything stored in his head, and just didn't want to show it. 'I see here that they did post-graduate work at Cambridge University in the same years, '64, '65. Were the two of them friendly then, that you remember?'

'Definitely not.' I told him why, even the '*arcistronzo*' bit. There seemed no harm in this, if anything the opposite.

But Carosi found harm. 'Neophytes,' he muttered scathingly, just loud enough for me to hear. 'Always the most dangerous. Take any extremist and you will nearly always find they are of recent conversion. It's practically a law of nature.'

'Then that lets Alberici out,' I said without reflecting.

But my examiner didn't take me up on this, he just smiled. A rare smile that made him look suddenly as if he might after all belong to the human race. Even if to a pretty poxy branch. 'It does indeed,' he agreed. 'It does indeed. If what I have on him here is correct, he would appear to have been a Marxist from the cradle.'

I didn't like the sound of that 'have on him'. What did he have on Sergio, I wondered? And from what source did he get it? And on who else besides did he 'have' things? On me as well? On all of us?

It didn't take me long to find out. I doubt he could have spoken to them all, not in that time, not without one of them at least braving the tapped line and ringing me up to tell me so, but Carosi seemed to know, not quite but almost as much about Lorenzo's and my circle of closest friends as I did. In factual terms, that is. He knew, just like he said, who they were, where they lived, what jobs they had and what was the colour of their political opinion. No, not colour, that was easy: tint, hue, saturation. And not only, he knew, besides, how they had got that way – the road that each had followed to the dye works, and the vat in which each had been soaked.

I was amazed and even frightened to listen to him – and on this, our second session, it was he, not me, who did most of the talking. Why this flaunting of his knowledge? Why this uncovering of his hand, when surely the wiliest technique for an interrogator is to keep his cards to his chest? What was his object? Simply to preen, to show his power for vanity's sake? No, that would be ridiculous. To cow me into submission by showing it? Not a very good tactic either. To show me someone else's power then: the power of the system, the power of the anti-terrorist squads or the secret services or whoever it was who had managed to glean all this inside information? That was more like it. But if so the ruse was self-defeating, because it was foolish information, foolishly gathered. Lorenzo and I weren't terrorists and none of our friends were either. I happened to be in a position to know that. And hence to know also that any organization that spent its time sniffing around these particular suspects was not well informed but badly informed. And therefore inept.

I think I said as much at this point, I couldn't resist it. Not only, but I think I dragged in the nationality issue as well, knowing how touchy Italians can be on this subject, and sort of hinted – perhaps actually stated – that a parallel investigation in England would have been a darn sight better run.

'Of course,' Carosi answered, smiling widely now, close on laughing. 'We can all see from the newspapers how smoothly such things work in the United Kingdom. No terrorism, no bombs, no victims, no IRA. Everything perfectly under control.'

I hated him so much I could almost taste the hatred, like heartburn in the back of my mouth. 'That was not what I meant, and you know it.'

'Do I? What did you mean? That the IRA is also far better organized, and that the British forces are therefore doing a better job *comparatively* speaking? Is that it?'

'More or less, yes.'

'Hmm.' The smile stayed on his face, but changed. I was beginning to know how to read his face for signs of emotion, or so I fancied. He leant forward, too, as he always did when he thought he had me cornered. Banal behaviour, in spite of all the sophisticated Jesuit frilling. 'I should be interested, Signora Gherardi, to hear how you came to form your opinion on the *modus operandi* of the IRA. Was it hearsay, or imagination, or was it direct contact? Perhaps you would like to tell me?'

I told him, as disdainfully as I could (which I flatter myself was pretty disdainful), that barking up the wrong tree seemed to be a generalized fault among Italian sleuths, and left it at that.

This narked him a bit, and when the interrogation was finished – if you could call it an interrogation: I'd been asked only a dozen or so questions, mostly about other people, and answered even fewer – we left on terms of outright hostility.

He pushed the notepad at me again for signing. I refused, saying I wanted to read what was written on it first.

He looked at his watch angrily and told me to go ahead and do so.

I tried but couldn't read his writing. In the end I asked rather feebly what the letters LCS stood for, which were about the only ones I could distinguish.

He told me, challenging my own disdain and if anything beating it, *Letto, Confermato, Sottoscritto.* Read, Confirmed and Signed.

When I still withheld my signature, I at last saw a warmish colour creep into his face. Not red, nor even rust, but a kind of foxy fawn. His blood – or whatever liquid he had inside in place of it – was getting up. 'You have not taken my advice, I conclude, and changed your lawyer?'

'No, I haven't.'

His jaw muscles tightened. 'I thought as much. Any lawyer with any concern whatsoever for his client would never advise them to cross the interrogating magistrate in such an unhelpful, childish way. Hinder me if you like, it is your prerogative, but not over silly formalities like this.' He snatched the block from under my nose and waved it at me. 'You sign this, I sign this, the clerk of the court signs it immediately afterwards to show he has witnessed the signing – that at any rate is the idea. A safeguard, no? A democratic shield to protect the rights of the individual against the mighty apparatus of the law?'

I nodded. I said I assumed, yes, that that was what it was.

'Well . . .' And he flicked through the empty pages, each of which had a signature already affixed at the bottom. 'The clerk has signed already, see? He's overworked, we're understaffed, so what does he do? He leaves me a dozen or so forms with the signature already in place, and I fill in the account of the interrogation afterwards, as I see fit. This is Italy, Signora Gherardi. This is not your beloved England, it is Italy. And this is how we do things.'

His frankness took me by surprise. No, not frankness, it was barefaced arrogance. I glared at him, even though the intimacy of eye contact wasn't pleasant to sustain. 'You mean I have no protection at all? That I am obliged to put my name to an account I can't even read, of questions you have supposedly asked me and answers I have supposedly given, knowing that you can alter it to suit yourself afterwards and make me say whatever you like?'

He glared back. 'You *can* read it,' he said. 'I've given it to you for that purpose. But please be quick about it. I too am overworked. Like the clerk.'

'No wonder there are terrorists. I've never understood

them before, but now I'm beginning to. When the system is so rotten . . .'

I might have used a swear word, from the force of his reaction. 'The system!' he threw back at me. 'The system! What in the devil's name do you mean by "the system", I would like to know?' Establishment, system, structure, base, platform, logic – logic of capitalism, logic of imperialism. This lazy leftist jargon – I'm sick of hearing it. Within this system you speak of there is a legal system, I will grant you that much, but if that is what you're alluding to then I must correct you: it is not rotten. It is disorderly, slovenly, chaotic even, but of the three powers of the constitution the judicature is the only one to conserve its independence and – yes, why not? – a fair degree of its integrity as well. There may be – in fact there almost certainly are – single rotten judges; there are lax practices, lax practitioners; there are delays, miscarriages of justice, a backlog of pending cases as big as Jupiter; but the system itself holds good. I wouldn't be in it otherwise, I wouldn't give my life to it the way I do.'

His first display of genuine emotion. And over what? A word, a carelessly used word. Soul of a pedant.

In the end of course I signed his wretched document, meek as a serf, but inside I was seething with resentment. He'd counselled me a lawyer, had he? No doubt thinking that without the family to advise me I would pick just any old hack of the forum. Well, I would surprise him: I would set my antennae working and single out the sharpest, toughest, rabidest bulldog of a lawyer to be found in the entire country. There was a group of young combative left-wing jurists known as Magistratura Democratica, which made a good starting point. I would find out from Sergio who he thought was the best of this bunch and engage whoever it was immediately. A rumpus with Elvira? Probably, but one more honestly didn't make much difference.

I said that during the interview Carosi's motives for giving away so much knowledge about Lorenzo's and my friends perplexed me. It didn't perplex me for long. When I called Sergio's office later that day from a pay booth and asked him to meet me at the Pincio in half an hour, I hadn't even the time to replace the receiver properly before the poison that had been so adroitly dropped into my mind that morning began to work.

God, I thought. Help. What have I done? Sergio was prime suspect at present among our closest cronies. Nothing more likely than that his phone was tapped as well as mine. The idea of him having contacts with terrorists was absurd, laughable, almost grotesque; but the police didn't know that. (And neither did I, come to think of it, not really, not the way I knew it about Lorenzo.) All they would know was that I had called him, furtively, from a public telephone, asking for a meeting and not specifying why. Enough – supposing he had, God knows, at some time of his life had a brush with even the outermost fringe of some terrorist group: a flanker of a flanker of a flanker, enough to put me behind bars for – how long was it Carosi had said? – thirty years, forty years. Oh, what was this quagmire I was getting myself into, and when, if ever, would I manage to struggle out?

I was shaking like a jelly by the time I reached the Pincio – a great shady belvedere overlooking the centre of the city, favourite fair-weather haunt of nursemaids and idlers, and today – a grey day – still pretty lively. When I saw Sergio, who was standing looking horribly conspicuous in the toddler audience of a Punch and Judy show, I was tempted to turn tail and run before he saw me. What if I had been followed? I had parked my car some way distant, in the lee of Villa Medici, and walked the rest of the way with my head practically back to front to check against just this possibility, but the police would be coming from a more central area – they might be here already, on the spot, waiting to clap handcuffs on both of us.

Idiot, I then thought. If that were so, then flight would be worse than going ahead with the meeting. And anyway, it was too late, Sergio had turned and was now coming towards me in huge strides. Looking, I must admit, in his dapper office pinstripe and Ryder and Amies tie, about as far from a terrorist as it was possible to imagine. (Although, wait, that was probably the way such people did dress if they had any sense.)

He bent down from his one-metre-ninety height to kiss me – I don't know what this measurement corresponded to in feet but it was outsize enough to have prevented him from being pall bearer at the funeral. We hadn't met since then and hadn't spoken, not properly, not beyond greetings and a few murmured words of sympathy, for longer still. In fact the last conversation I remembered us having had been over a pizza, and had concerned Bernadette Devlin's physical charms, or lack of: unless lured into one by anger, Sergio was one of those men who avoided serious discussions with women. Although I don't think I'd realized this fully till now, when, as he began to speak, I could sort of see him bending down towards me in a mental way as well.

'What is it, Juliet? Tell me, what's the matter? Why all this Hitchcock stuff? What is it you couldn't say over the phone for the benefit of our big-eared friends?'

'So yours *is* tapped. I thought as much.' I felt the flutter of panic lifting my diaphragm: I had only ever experienced it once before in my life, when at Montelupo there had been an earthquake and the house had swivelled under my feet as if a

71

giant hand had grabbed it and given it a twist. This flutter was lighter, and quicker to subside, but, still, it was a bad sign.

Sergio looked unconcerned. (Studiedly unconcerned, or genuinely so?) 'Of course it's tapped,' he said. 'It's the only thing they know how to do. Or *want* to do, anyway. Sit around on their arses in vans, with sandwiches and cups of coffee, and listen to Claudia asking her mother how to boil spaghetti, or to me, lecturing my clients about the snares of full-scale litigation. I should think they've tapped every number in your telephone book, if only you knew it, hairdresser included.'

Panic subsided, but suspicion stayed. A dirty rim of it: I wasn't even sure now I wanted his advice about a lawyer, I would just get one on my own accord – with a list and pin if necessary. There was something – I don't know – so dreadfully glib and artificial about what he had just said that I couldn't help commenting on it. And then regretting my comment, which sounded more artificial still. 'Surely Claudia knows how to boil spaghetti, doesn't she?'

Sergio gave me a look of surprise; alarm even. It was then, I think, that I was first consciously aware of the corroding effect of Carosi's poison: innocent or guilty, this particular friend of Lorenzo's was cut off from me from now onwards and I from him, and with the others it would soon be the same. 'Um, yes, of course,' he said quickly. 'I didn't mean literally. I was only . . . you know . . . giving an example. Only trying to . . .'

'Of course,' I broke in. And then in desperation launched into some wild explanation about how, when I'd first come to Italy, I'd thought all pasta had to be fried in a frying pan; and how in consequence it wasn't really so far-fetched to think that Claudia, who after all wasn't exactly domestic and had spent so much time in England, might also be a bit unsure when it came to cooking methods . . .

72

As the Venetians say of slapdash cobblers, the patch was worse than the hole. I'd have done better to stay silent. Sergio glanced about him nervously, and then up at the lowering sky and down at the dusty paving – anywhere but into the hectic eyes of his best friend's widow. Who was either dotty, or a terrorist herself, or else had formed some more or less unfounded suspicion about his own activities in that field; but who in all three cases it was better in future to avoid.

He tried a laugh, which came out nervous, too, and then took my fingers in his and brought them to his mouth, where he bit them gently, perhaps trying to make authentic contact. 'Juliet. Hey. Giulietta, Giuliettina. You didn't ask me to come here to talk about pasta.'

'No.' I decided to get things over with quickly, I could always ignore his counsel. 'I wanted you to give me the name of a lawyer. A good lawyer. For me. Someone to take care of me, follow just my concerns, quite separate from the family's.'

He blinked. I think he wanted to ask me whether my concerns *were* separate from the family's, but didn't quite like to. 'Isn't Russo good enough? Lorenzo thought pretty highly of him.' A pause while he registered my disbelief. 'As a lawyer, I mean.'

I shook my head and repeated I wanted someone of my very, very own. Adding that it was not my idea, either, but that the magistrate in charge of the inquiry had suggested it.

This appeared to rattle him more seriously than anything I had yet said. He gave a discernible start and tried to camouflage it by chasing away an imaginary insect. 'The Pubblico Ministero? Carosi? He thinks that? He told you that?'

I nodded.

73

'Well then, I would choose – let me see – someone like . . .' And he fired off three or four names in rapid succession, none of which he bothered to enlarge on and none of which I bothered to fix in my memory.

'Do any of them belong to Magistratura Democratica?' I asked, more for the sake of saying something than for any other reason. I was certain now that I must somehow choose my own man.

He looked faintly cross at what I realized immediately was my ignorance, and said that only magistrates belonged to that. Hence the name. Advocates could belong to the area, buzz around in the same political space, but they couldn't form part of the actual association. 'Otherwise it would be called Avvocatura Democratica, no?'

'Uhuh.' The awkwardness between us had grown into something palpable, like a sticky cobweb or a veil. I longed to get away but didn't quite know how to.

Sergio looked as if he felt exactly the same. And yet we had been close once – flirty together – often united by simultaneous attacks of the giggles while our soberer partners looked on bemused. Not any more. 'You could always go to the Palazzo di Giustizia and consult the rolls,' he said at length feebly, glancing around him again.

I latched on to this, pretending that it was a helpful idea instead of an exit line. 'Splendid,' I said in a deliberately chirpy voice. 'How do I do that?'

He shrugged. 'You just go there. You know where it is.' Then something – loyalty, remembrance, conscience – must have stirred in him, and he picked up my hand again, this time in a much tenderer fashion, and implanted a kiss on the knuckles. '*Che casino*,' he said in a sad voice. What a shambles.

I said nothing. The phrase he had chosen seemed to sum it all up: the mistrust, the fear, the distance, the silence that

74

henceforth we would not only have to, but actually prefer to keep.

'If you do go there – to the Palazzo di Giustizia,' he added, 'ask to talk to the President of the Order of Advocates. He's a trustworthy man – fair-minded; ultra, ultra correct. He knows the Roman legal scene inside out. If you tell him what you want in the way of a lawyer, he'll see you get it. And now,' with a shamefaced glance at his watch, 'I'm sorry, but I really must be going.'

I thanked him – making scant effort to disguise the hollowness of the thanks – and we said a hurried goodbye before quitting one another in relief. 'What's his name? The President's?' I called out over my shoulder as I walked away. 'Can I tell him you sent me?'

Sergio turned, and for a second I seemed to catch an expression of anguish on his face. I wondered if Franny's had worn it, too, when the cockerel had crowed for her. 'Afraid not,' he called back. 'I don't remember the name, don't even know the man at all really. Just ask when you get there; they'll tell you.'

CHAPTER SIX

My new lawyer brought with him, as far as I was concerned, new air, new hope, new everything. I went into the huge, grim precincts of the Palazzo di Giustizia with nothing inside me but Kafkaesque despair – how could I ever find my way through these scores of interconnecting courtyards, with their kilometres of corridors and cascades of staircases and flights of rooms branching off at every level and on every side? – and came out, miraculously, with more peace of mind than I had felt since the nightmare began.

The President of the Order of Advocates, once I had found him in the maze and outlined to him my requirements, was uncommunicative and brusque, but quick to understand my position. I suppose, what with the notoriety and everything, the case was quite a plum, and its bestowal, from the kudos point of view, not to be sneezed at. When I touched on the political qualities that I wanted my defender to possess, he hushed me up immediately with a spate of *Si, si, si, si, si's*, and *Certo, certo, certo's*, that made me feel I'd made a gaffe, or at least a gaucherie. But the message must have got through all right, because the three names he produced were all of them firebrand left-wingers. I checked them afterwards with Piero.

My final choice however was casual. With the slip of

paper in my hand I wended my way, Theseus-like, towards that part of the building where the full lists of members of the Order were kept, hoping to find there the addresses and telephone numbers of my three candidates; which the President had declined, obviously, to give, being far too grand.

The consultation looked like being complicated, and I showed the paper to one of the ushers, asking help in tracing the names.

'*Subito*,' the man said, hoisting himself anything but *subito* out of his chair. And then sank back again, relieved, and pointed to a thin figure in jeans and a fisherman's jersey who was crossing the marble expanse of the hallway in childlike spurts and slides. 'There goes one of them now,' he said. 'If you want to talk to him, this is a good moment to catch him.'

I lost no time, not even to ask which of the three I was pursuing, but dashed after the slider. When I caught up with him I pushed the President's note under his nose and asked – very rudely it now seems to me – which one he was.

'Number three,' he answered, unperturbed, indeed smiling his head off. 'Sastri. Paolo Sastri. Why? What do you want of me?'

And there it all began, and I began to breathe again and sleep again and eat again, and the shards of my life began gradually to look as if one day they might at last come together, ready for the glue pot.

Paolo – for so he became to me within minutes – lifted, as it were, the entire knapsack of fear and worry and solitude off my shoulders and placed it on his own. Willingly too, gleefully, as if he had been wanting just this burden to make his life interesting. Apart from Ubaldo (who was so bound up in Lorenzo his judgement hardly counted), he was the

77

first person to accept unquestioningly the thesis of the Neofascist plot. I didn't even have to outline it to him, either, or suggest ways in which we should try to prove it. His mind outran mine on every point.

He had known, he said, from the moment he read about it in the papers, that the official line of the 'accident while carrying out a terrorist attempt' was nonsense. Just as he had known about the anarchist Pinelli, fallen to his death while being questioned about the bombing in Piazza Fontana. Pinelli had never jumped out of that police station window of his own accord, no way, no way. And Lorenzo had never blown himself up. 'But we are pitted against a fierce, fierce foe, Giulietta,' he added. 'Oh, you cannot imagine how fierce he is. We will have to walk on eggs – you know the saying? – if we are to beat him.' And he performed an exaggerated little creeping step, like the cat, Tom, in the cartoon.

On eggs as maybe, but my new friend and helper walked fast. In the space of a few days he had already done all the things I had thought of doing and more – and far more thoroughly. He had picked the brains of a bomb expert, obtained from him in addition some rather shady-looking material on the subject of explosives, spoken to dozens and dozens of witnesses – practically all the employees of the firm, plus all Lorenzo's friends and acquaintances whose names I could remember. He had had a long talk with Nicolò, he had approached Elvira – from the right side, and then immediately, through no fault of his own, landed up on the wrong one; he had visited Montelupo and been shown by Ubaldo the places on which the *carabinieri* had concentrated their search.

Parallel to all this, or perhaps subsequently, or perhaps both, he had formed his own theory. Differing from mine only in that it was neater and more closely reasoned. The first question everyone ought to ask, he explained, in a case like this was, *Cui bono?* Who stands to benefit? If Lorenzo had indeed been a terrorist, what advantage would he have gained from planting a bomb in the outskirts of the little town of Rignano Flaminio? What could have been his possible targets? There was nothing close to the site of the explosion except the usual things like telephone wires and electricity cables, and these he could have intercepted at a far more convenient spot – Prima Porta, say, or Castelnuovo di Porto – driving only half the distance. The railway? Ah yes, well, that was of course the *carabinieri's* theory: the railway, with the handy intersection of road and line, and easy access from one to the other, and very little in the way of houses, or even traffic for that matter. But think carefully: it wasn't even a main line, it was just the measly little Roma Nord track, carrying commuters and the odd farm worker or two from Viterbo to the capital and back again at snail pace. Admitted the attempt had come off, how much coverage would a thing like that have got in the papers? A paragraph? Two? Half a column? Not even, probably just – yes – a couple of paragraphs, that would be about it. All that risk, and just two paragraphs to show for it at the end. No, even if my knowledge about my husband was nil and Lorenzo *had* been a terrorist, even then he would never have contemplated an action such as this, it was quite simply absurd.

What kind of terrorist, too, could he possibly have been? What kind of man? Because, make no mistake, the key question *Cui bono?* applied to the wider issue as well. Who were these terrorists with their bombs and bloodshed? Who were they working for? For the Right, obviously, and the Right alone. Creating havoc so that the whole axis of government could shift in that direction: towards repression, on the excuse of restoring order. It was a classic strategy, so blatant a child of three could hardly fail to grasp it. To sum up, therefore, a simple little hypothetical syllogism (or perhaps it was complex – his logic was getting rusty): if Lorenzo *had* been a terrorist, if he had really and truly been working for one of these shadowy groups, it would have meant he either had the political acumen of a toddler – no, not a toddler, a babe in arms – or else that he was secretly linked to the Neofascists himself. Was that possible? Was it possible I had been married for – how many years was it . . . ?

Seven. I told him. Seven years.

As long as that? *Complimenti*, I didn't look like an old married woman, not a bit. Was it possible I had been married for seven years to a political booby or a covert fascist militant? Or to both, seeing that they were practically the same thing?

No, I said, smiling despite myself. (He did me good, this man, he was – I don't know – he was wholesome, that was it.) No, it wasn't possible. Lorenzo was not only highly intelligent and highly politicized, but happened also to be the truest and best person I had ever known. Ruling out all three possibilities – stupidity, fascism and deceit. Sorry, I meant, ruling out *both* possibilities: I agreed with him that the first two were pretty much the same.

'That's what makes it so hard,' I added. 'Sitting in front of that wretched Carosi creature and having to listen to him refer to Lorenzo all the time with such contempt. I don't mind him despising me – I don't give a damn for his opinion. But I mind for Lorenzo. I can't explain, it kind of sullies his memory.'

Paolo dismissed this as irrelevant. 'You should try not to develop feelings of any kind towards the interrogating magistrate,' he advised. 'Not even ones of dislike. Remember, it's not a personal battle you're fighting, it's a political one. Who cares about memory? Win the political battle and Lorenzo's memory will take care of itself.'

I nodded. He was right, but it was easier said than done, not to dislike Carosi.

'He knows by now you're not involved, anyway. He must.'

Did he? Must he? I had endured two more interrogations since becoming Paolo's client, and I supposed that, yes, in a way these recent sessions had been less gruelling than the earlier ones. Just as unpleasant, but less gruelling. More boring perhaps. Carosi himself, definitely more bored by my answers. 'Yes,' I agreed, considering the matter. 'I think he does. I think you're right. I think he's coming round to view me as just a harmless cretin. Lorenzo a criminal fanatic, and me a cretin for not realizing it.'

Paolo's eyes twinkled even brighter than their usual. 'Ideal,' he said. 'Nothing better than to have the enemy underestimate your intelligence. Gives you a great advantage. When's the next meeting scheduled for? I forget.'

'Tomorrow.' My heart dropped at the mere thought of it.

So patently, too, that Paolo must have heard the bump. '*Coraggio*, Giulietta,' he said. 'Be brave. It won't last much longer, you know, this preliminary phase of the inquiry. Within a month at most the PM is required to come up with a decision: either he must request the opening of a formal inquiry or else he must opt for a dismissal of the case. He can't dither indefinitely.'

We were sitting outside as we spoke, on a wooden railing that enclosed the scruffy public gardens outside Paolo's office. We nearly always met and did business in the open, sunning ourselves, smoking, eating pumpkin seeds bought from a nearby barrow: he was that sort of person, Paolo – friendly, informal, easy to be with. I couldn't imagine what he looked like in his robes. A mess, I should think. Elvira was dreadfully scathing about his appearance, but then she would have found something to be scathing about anyway, no matter who I had chosen: she regarded my defection from Russo as a personal affront.

'What do you think his decision will be?' I asked. 'And what does it mean exactly, to institute a formal inquiry?'

Paolo's heart must have done a drop nearly as deep as mine did, but he disguised it better. He had already answered this question a shaming amount of times, but somehow the answer just wouldn't stick: it was the 'i' words again, it was as if I had no pegs in my head to hang them on.

'Well, forget about the technical side of things,' he said, super-patient as always. 'In practical terms it's a step ahead; it means we've got a case; we get a judge; our thesis of murder gets taken seriously.'

'Isn't a PM a judge? I thought it was the same thing.'

'No, a PM is more like a Public Prosecutor. What we get is a Giudice Istruttore. He is a magistrate like the PM, only the branch of the magistrature that he belongs to, instead of concerning itself . . .'

'Leave it,' I begged. 'I don't know what a Public Prose-cutor is and I don't want to know. Just tell me the basics: what you think Carosi is most likely to do, which option you think he'll go for.'

Paolo swung his legs up and left them sticking out at right angles, like a puppet's. His mannerisms were endearing; he really was the unstuffiest professional man I had ever come across. 'I think he will press for a dismissal,' he said, sounding very jaunty about it. 'I may be wrong. I may be wrong about *him* – some people say he is fair-minded, hard to influence. But my hunch is he has been put there for a purpose: to carry out a good old-fashioned *insabbiatura*. You know, when, like in the desert, the wind starts blowing and . . .'

I nodded. I knew what an *insabbiatura* was, I could hardly fail not to. All recent terrorist actions in Italy had ended up like that: the truth silted up under mountains of carefully accumulated sand. It was over two years since the disaster in Piazza Fontana, and only now were the investigators beginning to look in the right direction – and not very thoroughly at that, from what I'd read in the papers. 'So you mean it'll stop there? We won't ever know who killed Lorenzo?'

This was the outcome Russo had put forward to me as the most probable, and also the most desirable from the family's point of view; I couldn't help wondering for a second, if that was all that was going to happen, why I'd bothered to change lawyers at all.

Again my disappointment must have been obvious. (So that was why Carosi could read me so easily: I was like a wretched piece of glass. I must try for more sophistication in my reactions, I really must.) 'Of course it doesn't stop there,' he said, standing up with a jump and grabbing my hands in his, as if to transmit the current of his optimism. 'Not if we can help it. Carosi presses for dismissal, OK? – or perhaps he doesn't, poor fellow, perhaps we have misjudged him – but anyway, we'll presume he presses for dismissal of the case. What do we do? We press – that much harder – for the opening of a formal inquiry. We appoint ourselves *'parte civile'* – I don't know how to explain that one to you, but we ourselves bring the legal action this time. On behalf of Lorenzo. Against person or persons unknown.'

'Plaintiffs?' The term came to me in English from goodness knows where. Perhaps from a conversation with my father. 'We become plaintiffs?'

'*Forse*,' said Paolo, rightly dubious. Perhaps. 'But that is a weak word, it sounds as if it has to do with crying. We will

83

be strong. We will prosecute on our own account. We will become avenging angels, that is what we will become. We will lay siege to the Palazzo, we will challenge the whole system.

'Of course . . .' He paused and dropped my hands. I liked the no-fuss way he made and broke physical contact, it was very un-Italian in a man. 'Much will depend on the political orientation of the judge who is assigned. That we can't change, that we can't do anything about at all. But we wait, we hope, and then – *patapàmfete!* – we launch our attack.'

I asked him what our weapons were. It didn't seem to me, apart from the chiefly nuisance value of the left-wing press, that we had any. But on this point Paolo remained curiously cagey. I think he was afraid of the journalists getting at me and tricking me into revealing things by mistake. All he would do was to shake the folds of his baggy jersey at me and tell me not to worry and that he had an ace up his sleeve.

The official time limit may have been a month, but it was more than that before we had news of Carosi's decision.

I can see this from my newpaper cuttings. End of April. *'Caso Gherardi: richiesta l'archiviazione.'* A request for dismissal, just as Paolo had foreseen. And on the opposite page, taking up much more space, so you can see how Lorenzo's story is fading already in people's minds, a photograph of the stallion Ribot, dead at the ripe old horsey age of twenty.

Rita and Piero were having supper with me when the call came through: since Franny had fled and Carosi had sprinkled his poison, they were about the only real friends I had left; certainly the only ones in whose company I felt entirely at ease.

They absorbed the news with gratifying horror. 'The

swine,' Rita said, throwing back her hair in an angry parabola; she wore it long and crinkly as a badge of rebellion and often put it to dialectic use. Much more so than the head underneath, according to Piero. 'The stinking fascist swine. I hope he roasts in hell for it. Wonder if he did it off his own bat or if he's just obeying orders from the CIA or someone?'

Piero caught a strand of hair and sniffed at it fondly, but spoke directly to me, ignoring his wife's question. 'What did Sastri say? He's not going to give up here, is he? I mean, he's going to fight the decision? He's got the balls?'

I nodded and vouchsafed for Paolo's fighting spirit.

'Not balls,' Rita corrected. 'Say genitals. Or hormones. Something both sexes have. Balls I find insulting.'

'Not always, you don't,' said Piero, tugging at the hair. Their closeness saddened me. There was no one now with whom I could exchange silly banter like that. I was a monad, a sexual monad.

As best as I could I outlined Paolo's strategy. Piero seemed to think it rather tame, and said we'd have to flank it with a media campaign. He had endless journalist friends who were always interviewing me over the telephone and things, and talking about creating '*molto rumore*' and putting on pressure, but nothing much had come of their efforts so far beyond a few articles in the left-wing weeklies, harping on Lorenzo's commitment to social causes and showing him – rather unhelpfully, I thought – in a poolside photograph with a towel wrapped round him and a flower in his beard. Lord knows when it was taken or how it found its way to the press.

'Do we know yet who the judge is going to be? Did Sastri say?'

'No. He thinks he'll know tomorrow. Day after at the latest.'

'And then it'll all begin again. Poor you,' Rita said. 'Another swine to tussle with. But he'll never be as bad as . . . what d'you call him?'

'Pluto,' I said.

She laughed. 'Pluto's the dog in Mickey Mouse. You must say Plutone in Italian, or else it gives quite the wrong impression. Pluto is cuddly and has floppy ears; Plutone is all sex and sulphur. He's the one you want.'

I pretended, even to myself, that I hadn't heard: the connection between sex and Carosi was something I just couldn't stomach. I had never even once wondered whether he had a wife or was queer or neuter, or what he did for carnal gratification. Fish, I should think, if I had to settle for something: he buggered fish. Haddocks again, for preference after dessication.

However, the connection had been made, and that night – or probably it was morning because Rita and Piero stayed till nearly midnight, criss-crossing back and forth over their favourite ground of imperialist plots and cover-ups until I frankly got rather pissed off with them: they seemed sometimes to forget that the whole thing still hurt me like blazes – I dreamed Carosi was fucking me.

Fucking is not a word I normally use for copulation. I don't know why, I don't think it's prudery, it's just it doesn't seem to me to describe the sexual act very well – not as I know it, not as I practised it with Lorenzo. He and I screwed, we went to bed with each other, we made love; perhaps we fucked, too, but if we did we did it together, to one another. Whereas the Carosi of my dream did just that: he fucked me. He didn't rape me – I wished he had done, the dream would have been easier to deal with – he fucked me. Drive, drive, pound, pound, batter, batter; his body curved sort of backwards, away from mine, so that contact was reduced to a minimum and the prominence of the penis was all the more accentuated. I don't remember if he was clothed or naked, but I think clothed. He clothed, me naked.

Oh fuck. Really fuck – the swear word. I explored myself on waking to see whether my body had played me false as well as my stupid psyche, and found to my disgust that I was wet with secretion between the legs. Marco came into my bed for his morning cuddle and I could hardly bear to touch him, I felt so befouled. I knew it was stupid, and that the meaning of the dream had to do with power rather than sex, and that the dream Carosi was only a symbol anyway, not a person, but all the same I was ashamed. Randy widows: I was turning into cliché material.

Bice came to fetch Marco for his breakfast, and hurriedly, almost angrily, the moment they had left I masturbated. It was the first time I had done so – awake at any rate – since Lorenzo's death. The saddest sex I had ever indulged in, and the least rewarding. At the moment of climax I thought of explosions – Lorenzo had sometimes said that to me: 'Go on, explode; I'll make you explode,' and my mind leapt to the ripped-up tarmac and the hibiscus and the rest, and my pleasure congealed and ebbed away, and I was left feeling limp and shredded, like a burst balloon. My mouth felt sour, I felt sour, the whole of life felt sour; in fact I couldn't visualize it ever turning sweet again.

I twisted my face into the pillow and sniffed like an abandoned dog for traces of Lorenzo's smell but I couldn't find any, so I got up and opened his side of the cupboard – already bare of clothes, Elvira had seen to that, she had passed most of them on to Nicolò without even asking my opinion – and inhaled the air of that instead. If I hadn't feared the cleaning lady might hear me I think I'd have continued the beagle act and put my nose in the air and howled. Then, life being what it was, not sweet but rough and plaguing like a briar, the telephone rang, and it was Paolo with more news of the inquiry, and I was plucked back into practical matters again. Probably a good thing.

CHAPTER SEVEN

We were luckier with the judge than we were with the PM. The man was no left-wing sympathizer either, but unlike Carosi he seemed prepared to keep his mind open – wide enough, at any rate, and long enough for a little grain of doubt to be slipped inside before it shut again. He didn't seem to want me yet for questioning, either, not even in an informal way, which was a relief; he just went through the paperwork, did his pondering, and then in slightly under three weeks, which Paolo said was a record for a delibera-tion of that importance, granted our request and ordered the opening of a full inquiry. A slap in the face for Pluto/Plutone. A slap in that thin, dry, saturnine face.

It was Paolo's ace that clinched matters, of that there was no doubt. Without it, for all his detective work and zeal, our case was still woefully short on proof. There was a slightly mysterious telephone call that Giovanna, the secre-tary, remembered having put through to Lorenzo on the morning of the day he was killed, concerning some business matter or other, which she had omitted at the time to refer to the police because – so she said – she had been convinced for some reason that the caller was Marini; whereas now she was equally sure that it couldn't have been him, because the call was an outside one and she'd remembered having heard Marini's voice in the corridor saying something to someone about football only minutes later.

On account of Lorenzo's angry reaction to this telephone conversation – Giovanna said he'd told her afterwards some people would carve up your backside for prosciutto if you let them, and how was it he was always expected to be everywhere, do everything, from landing the commissions to ordering the cursed coffee from the bar – Paolo thought it possible, or at least arguable, that this call had been the ploy Lorenzo's murderers had used to lure him to his death. A fake errand, a meeting, a delivery – some pretext of the kind to get him on the road, bring him within their range. I tended to agree with him, but on instinct only. As evidence the whole construction was weak as straw, and both of us knew it.

Point No. 2 – slightly stronger, but not much – was a written report from the bomb expert, disputing the claim made by the police that the van had been at a standstill at the moment of the blast. The speed of an exploded vehicle, so the report stated, could often, it was true, be deduced from the wreckage, but only within a very limited range: fast, medium fast, slow, etc. There was no separating slow from very slow, and there was definitely no way of differentiating between very slow and stationary, the way the investigators had done in the present case. Which in turn meant that there were no grounds for asserting that Lorenzo had touched off the detonator himself; if anything there were grounds for asserting the contrary, since it was extremely unlikely that the driver of a moving vehicle, no matter how low its speed, would be so rash as to fiddle with explosives while at the wheel. Not to mention the related matter of the distance of the wheels from the kerb, which the police had affirmed could be calculated at x to y centimetres, giving additional proof that the van was parked at the time of the explosion; whereas in actual fact the margin for error in such cases . . .

It was all highly technical and highly notional, and I think on these two arguments alone – telephone call and speed – the judge would have brushed aside our objections and sent us packing. But fortunately, through a combination of luck and good connections and sheer hard work on Paolo's part, we did, as he promised, have the ace. Namely a four-minute sequence of film, shot for national news coverage but never actually shown, featuring a news reporter, standing not *at* but right *on* the bomb site, only a matter of hours after the explosion, holding up pieces of material to the camera and speculating on their nature and origin. Among them – in theory at any rate, and theory was enough – the detonating device on which so much of the PM's reasoning had turned. 'Ooohla!' was apparently the reporter's excited comment as he floundered around among the debris. (I refused to watch the film myself, still do.) 'I'm tripping over things here. There's bits everywhere . . . A chaotic scene . . . A scene of apocalyptic horror . . .'

Chaotic, or maybe not so chaotic. But anyway, unless someone went and destroyed the newsreels, which Paolo said was virtually unthinkable because so many people in the studios had seen them already, now we had a valid argument. It would have taken another Carosi to deny an inquiry in the face of such bungling, and, thank God or the devil or whoever it was appointed judges, the new man was not a Carosi.

Although Carosi was still around. I hoped we would be shot of him now, but alas not a bit of it. It was apparently his prerogative as PM, even though his request had been quashed and ours had prevailed, to be present at all the judge's sessions and to grub at will through all the relative documents. I didn't have to see him, thank goodness, at least not unless the judge changed his mind and called me for questioning, but I could still feel him there, hovering in the background – a murky little Bosch goblin in a corner somewhere, mucking up the canvas.

Towards the end of May, seeing that the inquiry looked set in its present form to drag on for the usual Italian span of months, perhaps years, I decided to go back to England for a week or two to see my father, taking Marco with me.

My Roman life had become – it's hard to describe it exactly – so empty without Lorenzo, so hard to live. No, empty is not the right word: there were dozens of things to do, but they were nearly all of them depressing. Reading documents, signing them, answering letters, answering the telephone, sorting out questions of inheritance with the repulsive Russo, and wrangling with Elvira over almost everything. From important things like Lorenzo's head-stone, which she wanted to be huge and ornate while I wanted it plain, down to the amount of toothpaste on Marco's toothbrush.

The opening of the formal inquiry had set a black indelible seal on our relationship. On her side she just couldn't forgive me for not accepting Russo's advice and letting things be. What did I want to go digging for? Why couldn't I realize that the less people probed into our family affairs the better? The facts; the truth; clearing Lorenzo's name . . . What a lot of pious nonsense. If there *was* anything to hide, I was playing right into the investigators' hands; and if there *wasn't* I was acting just as foolishly: keeping the wounds open; providing a target for the gossips, the *malelingue*. Was it possible I had lived seven years in Italy without grasping these simple, basic rules?

While I on my side couldn't forgive her her dreadful lack of faith – in Lorenzo first, but also in me.

Nicolò hadn't exactly helped matters either in this respect

by cornering me in the passage one afternoon and enfolding me in a tight embrace that at first, but only at first, felt like sympathy, and very soon felt like something quite different. I suppose it was part of the manhood manoeuvre that I'd predicted he'd have to make sooner or later, but I hadn't reckoned on it taking this form, and it troubled me and saddened me, even afterwards when I'd identified it for what it was. He said something childish and coarse about being 'bigger' than his big brother, and, besides tasteless and vaguely insulting, it struck me as yet another betrayal. What about that other time he had taken me in his arms – when I had felt so close to him and so comforted by the closeness? Had he felt like this about me then? Had that too been a camouflaged seduction attempt? Oh Nicolò. I prised him away gently, trying to make light of the whole episode, but as I did so I caught sight of Elvira at the far end of the corridor. She must have seen everything and understood nothing. Except that her daughter-in-law was truly the Messalina she had always suspected. Nor was there anything I could say to enlighten her without deepening her suspicions. Seducing her son, with his brother scarcely cold in the grave, and then throwing the blame on him, an innocent young man of not yet twenty . . .

Innocent. Uhuh.

Friends, as I said, were gone. Lost. Alienated. Only Rita and Piero left, and on the evening before I left for England I managed to quarrel even with them. Over the Calabresi murder which had just taken place the week before. Luigi Calabresi was the police official who had been conducting the case against the anarchist Pinelli, presumed at the outset responsible for the bombing of the bank in Piazza Fontana. It was he who had been questioning Pinelli when this latter fell to his death in the courtyard of the Questura; he who had been blamed for the death – either causing it purposely or through negligence, views differed – and he who had consequently brought down on himself, like a lightning conductor, all the opprobrium and loathing of the Left.

I came close to loathing him myself. I thought he was shifty and ambitious and ruthless, and had very likely done exactly what the left-wing press accused him of doing. I wasn't sorry he was dead, either, not on his account. I even agreed this must be yet another Neofascist killing, engineered to heap still more mud on the already well begrimed Communist Party. On all these points I saw eye to eye with my two remaining friends. But I couldn't go along with them in their dervish-like celebration of the death. Toasts to the unknown killer. Silly rhymes. Dancing round the floor with the cats, Tupa and Maros (why was it I had never realized before how daft these names were?): 'One less! One less! One *maledetto fascio* less!'

The television had shown his widow, a woman not much older than myself, coming to grips in public with the dreadful impact of her grief. They had given her Christian name: she was called Gemma; she was three months pregnant with her third child. Our husbands had been fighting opposite battles for opposite goals, and had I met her earlier we would have had nothing in common, probably, except strong two-way dislike, but now I felt a bond with her, so close that, had I known how to reach her, I think I would have stretched out to her in some way – sent a message, made a gesture. And I think she would have understood and made one back.

I tried to explain this to Rita and Piero but they were unsympathetic and if anything rather shocked. Politics and sentiment didn't mix, shouldn't mix. It was like a tennis match: once you started feeling sorry for your opponent, you'd had it, might as well hang up your racket and take up dressage. Of course I was bound to feel emotional – given the parallels and whatnots – but I wasn't to let it affect my political judgement: a dangerous enemy had been knocked out of the fray, and that was cause for rejoicing. If I had to think of widows, why didn't I think of Pinelli's widow? Bet she wasn't being so fussy tonight about who she drank to.

Next day as I drove to the station with Marco – Marini as usual at the wheel: Nicolò had offered to take us, but this time it was I who had refused – I felt as if I was leaving behind me no one I cared for, except for Ubaldo and Cesira. And possibly Bice, but I had been cross with her recently as well. Three employees. Three people who, fondness apart, shared very little of my mind.

Strangely, though, my mood rocketed as I climbed into the sleeper. I don't know why I had chosen to travel by train when flying was so much quicker, but I knew now it had been the right choice. For supper that evening, as we rattled through the shimmering riviera sunset, I put on a dark-red silk dress – my first attempt at elegance for ages – and walked into the restaurant car with a feeling, almost, of adventure. Life wasn't finished. I had taken a knockout blow, maybe, but Richard was something like himself again, and I was slowly coming round.

I look on that journey now rather as I imagine Christ must have looked on his days in the tomb: a rest period, a lying low, a hiatus between states. I found I could shelve everything, even my sadness – shove it up on the rack with the rest of the luggage and tell myself, 'Yes, OK, it's there, but you don't have to deal with it yet. Let it wait till you arrive.'

I allowed myself to be courted by a fellow traveller, bound for Paris. An amazingly stylish young sculptor with a grey-streaked ponytail (unworn by males in those days unless they *were* ponies), and an invincible fear of aeroplanes that I think he thought went to enhance his chic, and he was probably right. He confided to me his terror and his admiration, and I in return confided nothing but used him mercilessly as an entertainer for Marco. I flirted, sort of, with the waiters in the dining car. When I passed mirrors or reflecting surfaces – and there were naturally plenty of them on the train – I found myself glancing at my image with approval, sometimes even interest.

At Amiens, where we stopped and had to change, my make-up case fell open and all my bottles and stuff fell out on the line; and I counted, feeling rather smug about it, five male helpers, all of whom dived on to the tracks and squabbled for the privilege of retrieving my gear. Six with Marco.

The only sobering moment came when, on the ferry, and afterwards in the train to London, I discovered I had become the target for speculation on the part of two middle-aged Englishwomen. Proper Sussexy stuck-ups, by the look of them. Several times I caught them turning their well-powdered noses in my direction and mouthing things to one another over their Golden Arrow teacups, and I got quite paranoid about it, imagining they had recognized me from the papers and were discussing the bombing, probably branding me as a terrorist as well.

Not until one of them came up to me and pointed an accusatory finger and said, Pices (pronounced Paces), did the penny drop: they were discussing my birth sign, that was all.

I relaxed and laughed and said, No, Leo. But I'd have done better to remain paranoid and take the episode as a foretaste of what England had in store for me, because in fact I was received by nearly all of the very few people I met there as a kind of fair exhibit.

I'd forgotten what a taboo subject communism was in the

Anglo-Saxon world. Perhaps (like sodomy which I accepted straight off as a normal part of love-life) I'd never known.

My father's ex-valet and now factotum, Hunter, put me quickly in the picture, when he came to fetch me from Victoria. 'I'm sorry, miss,' he said, as we got under way, painfully embarrassed but evidently forced by manners to make some allusion to my loss. 'I'm sorry what those there communists went and did to your husband. Nice man, he was. Remember when we went after pigeons together. Good shot, too, for an Eyetalian. Shocking thing to happen, shocking.'

I thanked him, but felt I couldn't quite accept the condolences without some attempt at straightening the record. 'Only it wasn't the communists, Hunter,' I said. 'It was the fascists, the Neofascists. They are the ones who killed Lorenzo.'

'Ah,' he said, and I saw the back of his neck, already brick-coloured, turn an even deeper shade of red. 'I wouldn't know. Communists . . . fascists . . . But it'll be a bad day if ever either of them get a hold on things here. Bad fellas. Bad lookout altogether.'

I knew I ought to let the matter drop at this point, that it was more prudent and more considerate, but somehow I couldn't. 'That's a very narrow way of looking at things, you know,' I said, hearing the heat in my own voice. 'It may be different here, although I doubt it, but in Italy the Communist Party attracts some of the best people in the country. The most honest people, people who really want to see the end of corruption and the dawn of a just society.'

Hunter's head wobbled obstinately. 'I wouldn't know,' he repeated. 'I wouldn't know.'

'Yes, you would,' I insisted. 'Because I'm telling you. Lorenzo himself was a communist. And you've just said it, he was a good man. So. I am a communist. There's nothing wrong in it. Christ was practically a communist. Communism is a way of helping people.'

There was a sharp intake of breath but otherwise Hunter gave no sign of having heard. His neck went dark and rigid as a porphyry column, and the business of driving seemed to possess him utterly. 'I think I'll take the back way, miss, if you're agreeable,' he said after a little while.

I aimed my 'Fine' into the driving mirror, but he was looking resolutely ahead.

When we passed Windsor Great Park he glanced back into the mirror briefly, and I think, although it may have been imagination, that there were tears of emotion in his eyes. Pity, maybe, for the traitor I had become. Or shock. Or sorrow.

I felt suddenly sorry myself for having spoken. Lorenzo would have said I had done well to defend the Party image and open the eyes of a political innocent – he hated seeing working-class people adhering blindly to the Right, he said it was a double insult they suffered – but it struck me that, on the contrary, I had done something both unnecessary and cruel.

CHAPTER EIGHT

My father's attitude to politics was a little more sophisticated than Hunter's: he had been a diplomat for a while, before his early retirement, and in the scant time between the crossword and the bridge puzzle he read books on history and foreign affairs even now.

In a wry, understated way I think he'd been quite proud of the match I'd made, even after our disconcerting swing to the left that obliged him to change somewhat his version for family broadcasting. 'Juliet's millionaire husband seems to have gone and developed a social conscience. That's quite a smart thing to have nowadays in Italy, I'm told. Of course it'll cramp their style a bit – vodka instead of champagne, Russian caviar instead of Persian, that sort of thing. But no, seriously, they're in good company: they say the top echelons of the Italian Communist Party are composed almost entirely of plutocrats.' This was how he packaged the information for relatives and friends: as a joke but quite a repeatable one, referring to Lorenzo variously as My Stalinist son-in-law, or Che Gherardi or else the Bolshie Builder, and to me simply as the Poop. Short for Nincompoop.

This time, however, it was different. He seemed quite unable to deal with anything connected with Lorenzo's death that wasn't strictly, strictly personal. I found I could talk to him, that is, about my own sadness, and the family's reactions, and my difficulties with Elvira and things; even about financial matters and wills and property divisions and the difficulties these raised; but the moment I trespassed beyond, into the wider territory of the inquiry, and of friend and foe and guilt and innocence, he leapt away like an antelope.

'Daddy, you have a good legal brain, I wonder if I could sort of explain to you the way my lawyer is planning to conduct . . .'

'Ttt, ttt. Lawyers, Juliet, are paid for exactly that: to prevent us having to do the donkey work ourselves. Now. How about a game of backgammon, or has your son gone and lost all the pieces?'

'Daddy, tell me. Has Elvira been getting at you? Has she said anything to try and convince you that I'm doing the wrong thing in insisting on going ahead with the inquiry?'

'Hrrhm. What a suggestion. Elvira and myself are hardly on such intimate terms as to allow her to feel free to "get at me", as you put it. Whatever you are doing, I'm sure it's quite right. All I would suggest is a little more concentration on the task in hand: your queen is getting properly boxed.'

'Daddy, I need to talk to you for a moment. Seriously, just the two of us. I really do.'

'Certainly, Juliet. What about?'

What *about*? That really put the lid on it as far as I was concerned. In the end I felt like pinning him against the wall and shouting at him (all the better if in front of guests, only there weren't any of course because I was being kept segregated like the Glamis monster): Look! I'm a victim, for goodness sake. A political victim. The man I loved has been blasted to ribbons by an evil gang of quasi-Nazis, and you can't even bring yourself to talk about it with me because you find the whole matter indelicate. What is this idiotic English reserve? Of course it's indelicate. Death is indelicate. Murder is indelicate. Murderers are indelicate people. Bring things out into the open, for goodness sake; ring up your lady friend who I know moves back in here the moment I'm gone, ring up Aunt Imogen, ring up Uncle Ned. Ask them round. Let me talk to them if you daren't. I don't want to go creeping around with my head bowed as if I had something shameful to hide, I want to talk about things, defend my opinions, make sure everyone knows the truth. You, you're even reticent about Lorenzo. 'Ummm, errrr, always thought he was a bit of a hothead.' Well, so he was: his head burned – with ideas and indignation. Better a hothead like that than a cold junket-head like yourself. Caution, caution, quiver, quiver, what will people say? Who cares, as long as they say something, as long as this fusty veil of silence is swept aside and we get some light coming in.

I said nothing of the kind of course: it wouldn't have helped anyway. I did try once or twice to engage his attention over the fiddly little technical matters that his brain liked dealing with as a rule, such as the speed question and the range and accuracy of detonators, but even here I came up against the same hard rubbery wall.

'I'd leave those matters to the experts, poppet, if I were you.'

'But do you have an expert I could consult? Do you know anyone competent who could back up the opinions in our favour we've got so far? Anything like that would help.'

'Juliet, my love, I don't know if you've noticed, but my friends and acquaintances tend to be of a quieter disposition. I think catherine wheels on Guy Fawkes night are about their limit. No, I don't think I can advise you there.'

It wasn't just frustrating, it was worse, it was hurtful. I

had never been all that close to my father, except in rare moments over a gaming board, when, if I made a good move, I could see him thinking, Ah, flesh of my flesh after all perhaps; neurons of my neurons. But he had always been there in moments of need, with a handkerchief or a cheque book or whatever was called for. Even STs at a pinch. He had never turned his back on me, never overtly let me down. I could even remember, in a moment of extreme perplexity, asking him about sex, and getting quite a frank and almost too exhaustive answer: 'No, Juliet, it is not urine, not pee, as you put it, that the man introduces with his penis – that is the word, remember, penis – into the woman's vagina. Remember that one, too. It is sperm. S, P, E, R, M – a whitish, viscous substance containing . . .'

Was communism so much worse than sex that he couldn't handle it in the same textbook way? Was political assassination? They must have been.

Towards the end of my stay, not as a fresh-air policy I'm afraid but more as a protective measure against my cornering him, he began inviting in a few – carefully chosen – people. My uncle and aunt, the local GP and his wife, an ex-governess of mine who by chance had recently come to live in the next village.

After their visits (and fortunately during them as well: the Hunter lesson had sobered me a little in this respect) I began to see his point: these people effectively lived in a different world – a world of quiches and golf and old-fashioned roses and tapestry cushions. How could I sully it for them by introducing bombs and spies and other dissonant elements like these? Just by being there I sullied it enough.

The governess, Anna, couldn't even get Lorenzo's name right, it made her so twitchy, but confused it more than once with Leonardo. 'How was Leonardo's mother when you left? Such a well-dressed woman she seems from the wedding photographs, puts one quite to shame.'

The others were not much better. Cooler perhaps, but not much better. In fact from the way they all shied away from the subject while at the same time remaining intensely, almost morbidly aware of it, you might have thought that the bomb was still there in the middle of the sitting room, waiting to go off.

No, my stay in England, which I had intended as a break, a breathing space, was not a success. Except in the sense that I was quite relieved to get back to Italy again afterwards. As, too, I think, was Marco, who regretted only the return to black-and-white television. (Good thing, Lorenzo would have said. He despised consumer goods – most of them anyway – and didn't even hold with the drinking of Coca-Cola.)

On my father's face as he bent to kiss his grandson goodbye I saw the passage of a spasm, rather like the one that had crossed Sergio's when he had let me down over the matter of the lawyer. I think I was meant to see it, too, as it was still there when he raised his head. I looked deliberately down at the tickets in my hand: I wasn't going to let him cadge my forgiveness so late on and at such a cheap price.

'Keep in touch, beloved.'

Keep in touch? *Keep?* That presumed some kind of existing contact, and there hadn't been any, for Christ's sake, there hadn't been any at all.

CHAPTER NINE

Relieved to return to Italy, and then immediately not relieved. There were two photographers at the airport, waiting to snap pictures of me and Marco coming out of customs, and the fact appalled me. Two somehow was dreadful. A single one could have been the envoy of some dogged political correspondent or other, following a trial that remained hot for him alone; a larger number could have been the sign of a flare-up of interest due to some new development. Two, on the other hand, meant – or so I couldn't help thinking – that the story was being kept at simmer-level by the journalists themselves. Deliberately. Strategically. Because they didn't want it go off the boil, knowing that sooner or later it would afford more juice.

'Would you put your sunglasses back on, please, Signora Gherardi?' I was wearing them across my head like an Alice band: on, I supposed they looked more decorous. Widow-like. It seemed senseless to antagonize members of the press for so little.

'That's it, thanks.'

Grazie. Prego. Grazie a lei. All very civil and polite but inside I felt queasy, unsettled. Lorenzo, for all his apparent mobility, had been my pivot, my hinge, and without him I felt that one push in the wrong direction, and I could go careening off anywhere. Brakeless, rudderless, like an object in space.

Elvira welcomed me back emotionally: before I left there'd been some slightly huffy talk, mostly on my side, about finding myself a new flat. Now I was pressed to the spinnakers like the prodigal daughter and enveloped in a cumulus of Madame Rochas. 'You're home, *piccola*. You're home again. I'm so glad, I'm so glad.'

She meant it, too, while she said it: for all her absurdity she had a way of reaching the very centre of your heart – if she felt so inclined. 'Come into the kitchen straightaway, I have a little surprise for you. For Marco really, but, no, for you as well. Close your eyes, close your eyes. Both of you, that's right, and now give me your hands . . .'

And so saying she led us into the service area of the flat that she never normally visited, where the flip side of her welcome was awaiting us: a mongrel puppy, thin as a rake and riddled, by the looks of it, with parasites of every denomination under the sun. Under the earth, too.

I was so angry at the imposition that I think I literally shook. It seemed the meanest trick anyone could possibly play on me. No way of getting out of it either. Marco was already on the floor with his arms around the creature and a smile on his face I hadn't seen in a long while. 'Leo! Leo! I want to call him Leo. *Guarda*, Mummy. Look at him, isn't he *carino*. I bet he hasn't got a daddy either.'

'It's a she,' I said, my voice absolutely toneless. 'Put it down. It's filthy. And anyway it belongs to Nonna Elvira.'

Elvira gave me a look of mock surprise and then smiled a smile from which she was unable to erase a pleat of triumph. 'No, no, it's yours, Marcolino. Nonna Elvira would *like* to keep it, but she can't, on account of the cats. No, it's all yours. Yours and Mummy's. And you can call it Leo for Leonessa, which means a lioness, a lady lion.'

Impotence almost choked me. I loved dogs. I had always wanted to keep one here in Rome. But for some reason this one came – just as I knew Elvira wanted it to come – like a trap, like a fetter, like a live ball and chain around my ankle.

I knelt down beside Marco to inspect the wretched thing. 'Leonessa, eh?' Aware as I did so that already the door of the trap was swinging to.

'I thought you liked dogs, Giulietta.' Elvira spoke a little gingerly to tell the truth: she was not a dog lover herself, she couldn't really know the plan had worked until I had given formal capitulation.

I looked up, square into her face so that she could read all my rage, all my resentment, and didn't bother to answer.

What with vets and chemists and pet shops and all the rest, I don't think I got my unpacking done that night until after midnight.

Although you never know really with Elvira where the truth lies. Maybe I am maligning her; maybe she really intended her gift as a diversion. Her cats don't dig very deep into the crust of her life; maybe she thought it would be the same with me and a dog: something furry to strew on the sofa and stroke while watching telly.

But no, I think she knew all right. I think she thought, Responsibility, a shackle, a tie, ballast at the very least. Certainly what she never envisaged (and still less did I envisage myself) was that this mangy little creature would in fact lead me to greater freedom.

It happened like this. The inquiry dragged on and on, into autumn and the winter without anything to show for it whatsoever. With Carosi there had been a link – OK a nasty one, but strong enough for me never to feel cut out of what was going on on the institutional side of the fence. The new man, di Guido or whatever his name was, remained just that, an unclear name, an unclear figure, representing a process that seemed by now to evolve only in a two-dimensional world – words on paper, and cryptic words at that: dates, numbers, measurements, calculations, and endless references to codified laws, Article this, Article that. He'd said I could ring him whenever I liked and even gave me his home telephone number, but the one time I used it I got such a chilly reception I never tried again. I left the contact to Paolo, who was becoming embarrassed, I think, by the lack of headway we were making and tended also to be shorter on the phone than formerly. 'I'll be in touch, Giulietta. Trust me, the moment anything happens I'll be in touch. Until then . . .'

Only nothing did happen. More experts were consulted. *Periti* they were called, and they came up with what were called *perizie*. Each *perizia*, even the ones we ordered ourselves, took a fantastically long time to concoct, and once it was ready it appeared, like the hydra, automatically to elicit a blossoming of other *perizie* that took even longer. As a stalling device it was as refined as the mechanics of a Mafia killing, in which the victim is so trussed by the ropes that in the end he executes himself. I tried desperately to bend my own mind to the implications of each new opinion as it came in, but it was like tussling with some ghastly geometrical theorem: if A is the target and B the assassin, then AB is the trajectory of the electronic impulse, and if S1 is the speed of the impulse and S2 the speed of the vehicle, then the speed of impact is to be seen as lying with the range S1+S2 and S1–S2. In order to calculate, therefore, the value of AB in the case where S1=X and S2>0 . . . Hopeless. And to make matters worse, all I could really see in place of the signs and figures was a road and a van and a hibiscus, and Lorenzo driving along unawares towards his death.

From the hell of the first month I appeared to have landed

up in limbo, and I honestly was hard put to say which was worse. Rita and Piero were tireless in their efforts to keep my spirits up – constantly inviting me round, introducing me to new people, re-hashing my story time after time and refusing to allow the collective indignation of their 'progressive' friends to cool – but in the end it got so that the sheer magnitude of their effort depressed me, and, bitterly ashamed, I begged to be left alone. (They took even this rebuke with generosity: suffering is bad for you in that way, it allows you to get away with all kinds of rudeness.)

My days were spent with Marco and Bice mostly, on the tranquillizing plateau of childhood occupations. Playground in the mornings, ditto in the afternoon if it wasn't raining, children's telly in the evenings and then supper and stories before bed. But even this safety routine had its hazards, inasmuch as the area where we lived was small and gossipy, and if ever I accompanied Marco to the playground myself instead of Bice, the other children would melt away on the instant in Pied Piper fashion, leaving him isolated like a leper. No scurrying, no fuss, no shouting of mothers, nothing: his playfellows of ten seconds earlier would simply not be there any more, that was all.

The dog, therefore, fitted into the pattern of our lives like the missing piece of a jigsaw. I would drive to the park, dump Marco and Bice – the two innocents of the piece – at a certain distance from the swings and whatnots, drive on to the wilder part, leave the car, and away I would go. No longer alone but in the company of, one, an ugly little ginger bitch with a terrible figure, and two, a most beautiful blond-haired girl of roughly my own age, slightly younger, with the most alluring figure I had ever seen.

I met her the second day I went there, and she showed me – as a friendship offering, I suppose, having little else at her disposal – all the secrets that this rather dodgy part of the park had to offer.

She knew it inside out – far better than I did, who had lived on its perimeter for the past five years. She knew a bit of its history, too – the families it had belonged to before coming under the grasping paw of the Savoias, and then down through them to its present owners. (Although perhaps not outright owners. She was a bit vague about how things stood now: there was some kind of law suit pending: the *Comune*, who wanted to effect a compulsory purchase, and the family, who still lived in the villa right in the middle, trying to hang on. Other wanderers at their peril like ourselves said there was a prince who roamed the interior with a pack of mastiffs, discouraging trespassers, staking out his rights.) Anyway that was how the park had acquired its present character: its mixture of grandeur and ruin. That was why you came across all these exotic trees, bound around with bryony and brambles and stuck with junkies' syringes. That was why the foxes ran loose in it and tramps lived in the follies, and truants from school lit fires in the empty fountains. It had been up in the world about as high as a park could be – Versailles-level – and then it had gone dramatically down.

The girl, Valeria, said all these things with such love of the place that I was ashamed. Ashamed at myself and enchanted by her. The first week or so I hardly dared make an appointment, the fact of our meeting seemed so delicate that I was afraid if I rushed her she might disappear. Into a tree or something, like a hamadryad. She had a lot of the wood-sprite about her, and I recognized that immediately, even before I knew about the prison in which, like Ariel, she was entrapped.

To begin with we didn't talk much. I would watch out for the little red Fiat station wagon that she drove, and for her tall striding figure with the camouflage suit and green Wellingtons, and the wolf-like Alsatian that loped along beside, a pinecone invariably stuffed into its rather goofy jaws, and once I had spotted her I would just give a wave and then join her and tag along behind. We had to walk in Indian file because the paths through the undergrowth were so narrow, and she had to go first, because I didn't as then know the way. The many, many ways.

This was probably what saved us from the friendship point of view, for if we had talked so early on we would doubtless have fallen out immediately. The moment I had said who I was she would have snorted at me with those flared nostrils of hers and told me I must be crazy. '*Baccalà!*' she would have said: codfish – it was one of her favourite terms of abuse. 'Stupid codfish!' And then she would have opened her mouth and made that feeding gesture with her hand that she had picked up from her *Romanaccio* boyfriend (man friend, rather: he was well over forty) to signify that I would swallow anything.

And I? Without her story, I would have just dismissed her as a prejudiced bourgeois bitch, as rapacious and empty-headed as her own Alsatian. She spoke such good Italian and was so familiar with the city, not only the park, that I think I might never even have realized she was a foreigner like myself.

Instead our friendship developed along its own lines, in its own way, so that we were bound to one another by, if not love, then something very close to it by the time the differences surfaced. (Need, admiration, and a kind of giddy acceleration of the heartbeat in the other's presence: those are the ingredients I can boil it down to on my side.) Every rainless day for – it must have been a good three or four months, perhaps longer, we met and walked. Mostly mornings, but sometimes, when Marco was fixed up with friends, afternoons as well. We had adventures together. One day we met a madman who was hitting trees and got into a fight with him – before, that is, we realized he was mad. The dogs were hopeless – just stood by and wagged their tails while this huge, stick-wielding figure attempted to push us both into the lake. It was really scary while it was happening, but afterwards, when for some reason the man suddenly wheeled round and left us and went back to smiting his trees again, we were overcome by laughter. We lit up cigarettes and choked on the smoke, and rolled over on the grass with our feet in the air. 'Stop that!' Valeria shouted out at the top of her voice (imitating my first bossy intervention with the maniac that had got us into all the trouble). 'Trees are living things, you know. Their bark is like a skin.' Foolhardy perhaps – the man was still within earshot – but it struck us both as the funniest line we'd ever heard and we went on shouting it until our stomach muscles would take no more.

We met the prince, too, and his nine Neapolitan mastiffs. No myth, but whiffling, slobbering and potentially quite dangerous reality. And again our trustworthy dogs let us down and bolted, and again, when the scare was over, we lay on the dry leafy floor of the wood and wet ourselves, practically, with mirth.

Once, when Nicolò took Marco to the seaside for the day, we picnicked in one of the glades and then basked until sunset in the hazy bronze Roman air, the dogs panting under the pines, disgusted by our inactivity.

Grave political things were happening around us all the time. A car bomb went off near Gorizia in the north of Italy, killing three *carabinieri* – a terrorist action of clear right-wing matrix. In Germany Andreas Baader and Ulrike Meinhof were captured, and the matrix that had turned them out was not so clear: Rita and Piero and all their set slid round the problem by dismissing the pair as *'fanatici'* and decreeing that Germans, even when they were avowed Marxists, were always Nazis at heart, but for me it was the first intimation that terrorism could indeed be red, and I hardly knew what to do with this piece of information, whereabouts in my head to store it. Then there was the terrible bombing of the Olympic Village in Munich, and street-fighting in Santiago, where the Allende government seemed to be on the verge of toppling. Yet my dog friend and I never touched on any of these topics in our conversations – almost as if we knew the time was not ripe.

The day Valeria – still striding ahead, not looking at me at all – suddenly embarked on her life story, and spewed it all out, the prison, the attempted rape, the year's detention and all the rest, it was something quite different that sparked her off. Something trivial, personal; I don't remember exactly what but I think it might have been something to do with going to the lavatory.

Yes, that was what it was, how could I have forgotten. She said she had to pee, and while she was peeing she said, 'Blast, it's not only pee, I've got to do something else, pass me some leaves – nice thick ones.' And still managing in some extraordinary way to look elegant, attractive and not in any way at a disadvantage, she evacuated right there on the path, clinging on to the dogs' scruffs for balance, and then stood up and righted her boiler suit and resumed her walk.

I expressed surprise – more, admiration: there were several other walkers out that day, and the thought of being caught squatting, crapping, naked to the waist, would have blocked me completely.

'Ah,' said Valeria. 'Yes, well, you haven't had my practice.' And that was when on her side the reserve broke down and she began to talk about herself.

She was Hungarian, from Budapest. A doctor's daughter, brought up in a family that for heritage, brains and traditions still considered itself privileged. At nineteen, beautiful, irrepressible, top of her class in every subject, she had won the prize of a journey to Italy, along with twenty other outstanding students of her year.

They had toured various regions, enclosed in their bus like goldfish, and then – a prize within the prize – they had wound up in Rimini of all places and had been granted a few hours' freedom to walk along the beach.

Valeria said she thought she acted without thinking, but that afterwards she revised her opinion and decided she had been thinking all along: watching from her seat in the bus the carousel of this sunlit and joyous country as it spun before her gaping eyes, and waiting for the moment she could slip out and join the revellers.

She did just that. She got chatting with some boys on the beach, one of whom had a motorcycle, and when she felt no one was looking she swung her leg over the saddle of the bike and told the boy to drive off.

He obeyed her, and she never came back. For nearly a month she lived a carefree, beach-and-villa life, staying with whoever had a spare bed and easygoing parents who asked no questions. The group she had got into were the sons and daughters of professional people – plenty of money, wildish, but all things considered nicely behaved, and respectful of her as their peer. They housed her, fed her; the girls lent her clothes and make-up, and the boys petted with her only an ounce or two more heavily than they did with the females of their own set. One of them got quite soft on her and turned protective. Apart from the worry of not being able to ring her parents and let them know what she had done, she had a really good time while it lasted.

'I knew my mother would know, anyway,' she explained

to me when I questioned her on this point, 'because we are so alike. In my position she would have done the same. She told me so afterwards. She never blamed me, never held it against me, never even criticized. Snatch at it, was all she said. It's your life, go for it, snatch at whatever it has to offer. Of course,' voice getting a little sadder, 'certain things I've never really told her, not in detail, not over the phone.'

The 'certain things' didn't make very happy telling. Towards the end of the bathing season, just as Valeria had begun to sober up and address the problem of what to do in an alien country, without work, without papers, she and her motorbike pal had been stopped by the police for a random check. Her illegal status had come to light immediately, and her friend (the hitherto protective one) had dropped her faster than a lighted squib.

Under police escort she was then taken by train to the frontier with Austria, where there was some kind of refugee camp for fugitives from Eastern Europe, and literally turned out on to the rails and told to walk across the divide.

Once across she was arrested and sent, not to the camp, but to an ordinary prison. She spoke no German. Her requests for an interpreter were misunderstood or, she suspected, wilfully ignored. She was put into a cell with two common criminals, one of them a butch lesbian with an outsize male member tattooed on the inside of her thigh, which she flexed at Valeria on entry, in presence of the guard; the other a semi-demented individual, given to screaming fits and accused of child abuse. There she was left for a period she couldn't remember but which seemed to her in retrospect close on five days before receiving attention of any kind. Beyond the attentions of one of the prison guards – old, male, repulsive – who watched her through the spy-hole when she used the lavatory, situated, unscreened, in the corner of the cell.

Her period came during this time and she was obliged to mime to this man her need for sanitary towels, her cellmates having laughed and shrugged their shoulders. He laughed, too, then appeared with some magazines and watched as she tried to make use of them.

One night she awoke to find the cell empty and the guard – this guard – standing by her bed, in the act of unbuttoning his trousers. He threw himself on her the moment he saw her open her eyes, but by some miracle she was quicker, drew her legs to her chest and then pounded them at him with all her strength, catching him in the midriff and hurtling him to the floor.

He broke an arm in falling. For this Valeria was taken before some prison official or other and, unable to give her version of events, was put in solitary confinement for a month. She said she was better off that way. The only thing she dreaded was the daily walks in the open, with the other prisoners staring at her and jeering and shouting things she couldn't understand. For this reason she stopped going out, and when finally at the end of the month she was granted an interview with the governor in the presence of an interpreter from the Hungarian Embassy, she had grown so unaccustomed to daylight she had difficulty in seeing.

The interpreter must have been quite shocked by her plight; perhaps the prison governor also. That same day she was released and sent to the Refugee Centre. Here there was quite a colony of Hungarians awaiting decisions, placements, documents and so forth, and she slotted in to this group automatically, having no other choice.

Life was hard there – harder than her prison confinement, Valeria said, only not quite as hard as life in the communal cell. Strife, jealousy, in-fighting: her fellow Hungarians were a rough, competitive lot and made her pay for being a cut above them on the social scale by keeping her in a tight margin. No favours, no friendship, no warmth – they merely endured her the way a pack of wolves endures a lone intruder. She made only one friend among them, a girl slightly older than herself, who was likewise marginalized on account of having got herself pregnant: a weak move in such taxing circumstances.

This girl, and the child she was carrying, became the focus and fulcrum of Valeria's life as an intern. After her first few months in the camp she was able to obtain a day permit for work outside, and got a job in a ski factory, assembling skis. The pay was low but it kept the two of them, and then the three of them, in clothes and food.

'I was the breadwinner, the husband,' was the way she put it. 'It made me feel strong and useful. It kept me going.'

'Didn't you ever think of packing it in? Going back to Hungary and your parents?'

'Are you mad? After all I'd gone through?'

'But the dream – the dream of the West, and freedom, and plenty – you knew that wasn't real any more?'

'Did I?' Valeria said. 'I'll tell you something. They used to make us read a lot of Russian books in school. Tolstoy and stuff. Classics. Well, you know one of the things that struck me most? It was that scene in *War and Peace* when Natasha and Sonya are getting ready for the ball. I don't know, I just thought to myself how it was one of the happiest-making things in the world: the idea of two pretty young girls getting ready for a dance – choosing their clothes, doing their hair, prancing around in front of the mirror chattering together and trying things on. The smell of freshly laundered clothes. Scent. Powder. Mothers watching maybe, aunts, nurses. Everything very feminine, lots of bustle, and a kind of sexual thrill running through it all. You know what I mean?'

I could see Lorenzo's face in front of me, his mouth

116

curling with disgust at such a typically bourgeois fantasy, and had to pause a moment and inspect my real feelings before giving my answer. 'Yes, I know what you mean.'

'Well, think of a world where you, a young girl, are shut out of the scene on account of your birth or poverty or something, OK, but the scene still goes on. And then think of a world where you're shut out because there aren't any balls; where everyone is shut out, not only you; where that scene, that brilliant, happy scene, is no longer enacted. Which is worse? Which world is more depressing? Which is the one you would choose to live in?'

I still don't quite know how I would answer this question myself, but Valeria plumped for the ballroom and her peep-hole in the maids' gallery. She worked a full year in the ski factory before she won her freedom from the Refugee Centre. Then, with a temporary 'guest-worker' permit and friend and baby still in tow, she moved to a rented room and began looking around for a better-paid job. The only thing she was offered was work as a waitress in a bar. She accepted: longer hours but more money, more company, and tips. In the bar she eventually met a man who fell in love with her and asked her to marry him. Her friend having meanwhile drifted back into the relationship with the father of the child and moved elsewhere, Valeria accepted this offer, too.

The marriage was stormy and disastrous. The man – still a boy really: he was only twenty-two – was given to drink and spells of violence. Valeria took in a kitten to keep her company and he slew it out of jealousy, depositing the body on her pillow. He beat her up regularly, every time he was drunk, and poured pitch on her clothes so that she couldn't go out.

She ran away from him – literally so, rushing on foot to the station with her few untarred belongings and leaping on the first train bound for Rome. (Italy was still in her mind the sundrenched and welcoming land of her first encounter.) This time she had a valid Austrian passport and got work as a freelance translator without much difficulty; only her German was still scrappy and translations into Russian and Hungarian were not in great demand, so life was still pretty tough. Every month she had to report to the Questura and request a renewal of her entry permit, which could be denied at will.

It was then, after she had been scrabbling along for several months on pasta and Nutella and her meagre translator's earnings, that she met Marcello, the man she lived with now. He had sorted her out immediately: on the permit front he had arranged for her divorce from the cat-killer and then, for the modest sum of half a million lire, for her instant re-marriage to an old-age pensioner, who she only saw once, briefly, at the wedding.

'I'm a widow now,' she said, throwing back her river of golden hair and smiling a funny little self-deprecating smile. 'So it couldn't have worked better. Except I suppose the name could have been a bit . . .'

'A bit what? What *is* your name?'

The smile widened with real amusement. 'Sturabotti,' she chuckled. 'I'm called Signora Sturabotti – the Widow Sturabotti. It means a barrel cleaner, someone who scrapes out barrels.'

'Won't Marcello marry you himself some day – now there's the divorce laws?'

An ingenuous question. Marcello was a wholesaler of domestic appliances – a blustery, self-made mini-tycoon, with a wife and family. Valeria was his mistress in the old-fashioned sense of the word. He had set up house for her, furnished it with demimondaine frills and flounces – down to a bevy of furry animals in pastel colours lolling along the sofa top. The car, too, was his present. He bought her jewellery and couture clothes, though mostly for inside wear. (The Alsatian was an oversight, a mistake on his part: he had promised a dog and allowed Valeria to choose the breed.) He visited her regularly, twice a week, Wednesdays and Saturdays, and insisted on her close observance of ritual on those days: freshly shampooed hair, shaved legs, black underwear, no, absolutely no telephone calls from those few acquaintances he allowed her to go on seeing. She must cook him dinner, too, but early, as the flat must smell of scent, not cooking.

The rest of the time was her own, and it hung heavily on her jewel-laden, manicured hands. Hence the dog, hence the walks. Hence our meeting.

I asked her if it was worth it. All along, as I followed the unravelling of the story, it was this question that lay in the back of my mind. And pressed on the front of it, too. Could her life in a communist country really have been so bad as to make these ordeals (of which quite honestly the present one didn't seem to me the least) seem preferable? If so, then what had we been striving for, Lorenzo and I? What in the name of Marx and all the Party bigwigs had we been striving for?

'*Baccalà*,' she replied, gesturing first at her own elegant person and then up at the shafts of winter sunlight streaming through the ilex trees. 'Of course it was worth it. *Baccalà*.'

CHAPTER TEN

The new year brought me at last a summons from di Guido. Informal: a little *chiaccherata* he called it, a little chat. Would I mind if the Pubblico Ministero was present? I could easily refuse if I wished – the PM only had the right to sit in on formal sessions – but I knew how it was . . . refusals put people's backs up. It wasn't as if he and I had secrets to discuss; all he wanted to do was to put me in the picture, let me know the stage the inquiry had reached. I wanted to consult my lawyer first, did I? By all means, go ahead and do so. But please to communicate my decision quickly because they were all of them, judges and magistrates, on a very tight schedule.

'Ski-ing season,' Paolo said tersely when I rang him. 'Lawyers work, judges do nothing at all, most of them. Now is the time they set off for the mountains with their wives and broods. Often they are prolific, must go with the mentality.'

'Is Carosi prolific?' I can't think why I asked that, the answer didn't interest me in the slightest. Or did it?

Paolo hesitated. 'Not sure,' he said. 'One child, I think. Perhaps. Unhappy marriage, though. I seem to remember Madame Carosi ran off with someone else – a colleague. Promiscuous lot, too. It's the high pay and all that spare time.'

'Can't say I blame her.'

The night before the meeting I couldn't sleep, and when I finally got off I had another Pluto-infested dream. This time it wasn't sex – not explicit sex, that is – but it was still harassment, unwanted intimacy. I had some household problem – shelves that kept falling down or something of the kind – and Carosi appeared with an electric drill, held at groin-level, and began making holes all over the place: in the furniture, in the bedclothes, even in the mugs, so that when I had my breakfast coffee it shot out from the side in a stream, all over my hand. There was no stopping him. I called to Ubaldo, but Ubaldo for some reason refused to be involved. Worse, he put his arm round Carosi's shoulders, friendly as could be, and led him over to the old-fashioned hand plough that sits rusting at the bottom of the orchard and started showing him how to use it. I awoke to the sounds of road workers in the street below and to the vision, still in my head, of Carosi drawing a furrow though my prized rhubarb patch.

Translated into reality my dream driller was his reserved and gelid self, sitting right in the corner of the room, bent over his papers, a pair of Raybans darkening his already Stygian features: his only concession to weakness a little smirk of I-told-you-so satisfaction as di Guido admitted total stalemate in the investigations.

I couldn't believe all this delay wasn't deliberate stalling. 'But the newsreel footage?' I urged. 'Doesn't that prove something? Doesn't it give us some kind of lever? I thought you said . . .'

Di Guido reached for his asthma puffer: he was the direct opposite of Carosi in physical terms – pink and wet and rheumy. Spongy-looking. 'It proves very little,' he sniffed, 'except that our police department is not Scotland Yard.

Things were not well handled; they seldom are. Bits of evidence were tampered with by error; this happens all the time. I have a case on at present – a murder case – in which the entire corpus of proof is missing. No evil intent, that we can make out: the police detectives took their samples from the scene of the crime the way they always do, put them in their little regulation plastic bags, sealed them tight, sent them to the lab, and that was the end of the matter – they never arrived. Who can say what happened to them *en route*? Whether they were lost, or stolen, or sent to the wrong department, or simply ended up as cat food. Boh?'

I found this a pretty tasteless way of speaking in the circumstances, and to do him justice I think Carosi did, too. From his corner I heard him make an angry-sounding cough.

'But we know what happened to our evidence,' I insisted. 'We've got evidence of it.'

The phrasing was clumsy. Di Guido smiled. '*Prove delle prove delle prove*,' he intoned in a sing-song voice. 'No, Signora Gherardi, I'm afraid you must arm yourself with patience. We have more reports coming in shortly. On your lawyer's request the remains of the electronic detonator have been sent to America for expert examination. Who knows, perhaps their Perry Masons will come up with some theory that will enable us to clear your husband's name. Massachusetts Institute of Technology and all that. Very clever people.'

Automatically I corrected his pronunciation. 'Massa-*choo*setts.' It was the first time I appeared to have awakened his interest in anything I had said.

'Is that so? Massa*choo*setts? Ah.' And he made a note on his up-till-now virgin pad.

I felt like shaking him. 'What about that strange telephone call my husband received the morning he was murdered?' To my shame I had completely given up trying to follow the ins and outs of the explosion and everything that hinged on it, but the telephone call was more accessible, and perhaps for that reason I had given it recently a certain amount of thought.

Di Guido looked at me balefully. 'You mean the morning your husband lost his life. We don't know yet that he was murdered, do we? That is what we are here to establish.'

After this there was little left to be said. The usual, We will notify you, We will be in touch. On my way out I passed close to Carosi's chair and he rose a couple of millimetres and gave a mocking little inclination of the head. Things were undoubtedly going just as he wanted them: another six months or so and this colleague who had replaced him would be winding up the case in exactly the same way he had recommended himself – dismissal for want of proof.

Only it was want of will, not want of proof. The general will, like in Rousseau. Elvira would be relieved, the whole family would be relieved, probably by then political supporters and journalists would be relieved, too: they could write Lorenzo off as a dead loss in all senses and transfer their zeal to some other more promising victim. I was the only one who would go on smarting under the injustice of the affair, but I would smart alone.

Later that day, to blow the frustrations out of my head, I went for a long windswept walk with Valeria and told her everything. Tipped all my skeletons out of the chest – just as she had done with me.

It was like putting conditioner on tousled, knotted hair, the result was so soothing. 'So you're a widow, too,' was her first response. 'Two widows. Merry widows. Da da da da *dum*, da *dum*, da *dum* . . .' And she grabbed hold of me and whirled me round in a waltz.

I had never concealed from her my political opinions, such as they were, but I had never really discussed them with her either. Now I tipped them out, too. After months of her company, and of hearing her decry the system in which Lorenzo and I had placed such hopes, I could see that they were in the most terrible mess.

She listened patiently, however, far more patiently than Franny, and far more sympathetically than the *carabinieri*. At the end I expected her to make some comment, probably scathing, but she just waved her hand like someone brushing crumbs off a table and asked me about Lorenzo instead.

'What was he like, this man of yours?' she said. 'This rich communist man with a priest's conscience, what was he like?'

The description struck me as strangely apt, coming from someone who'd never met him. 'Just like you said: a rich communist man with a priest's conscience.'

'Yes, but what was he like to live with? What did he look like? What did he dress like? How did he treat you? What did he like doing in the evening – seeing films, watching television, going out, what?'

For perhaps the first time ever – I don't remember even doing it for my father when we got engaged, although I think he might have appreciated it – I found myself painting from memory a portrait of Lorenzo. So scrupulously, too, and in such detail, that it was almost as if I was making the likeness for myself, as a keepsake.

Curious little aspects of his character came into my mind – things I had forgotten, things that maybe I had never really known, or not consciously. The way, for example, that he liked me to dress: outwardly unconventional, but at the same time with all the hidden conventions slavishly respected. 'Your legs are looking a bit furry, Julie, shave them, get them waxed.' 'What's this rag you're wearing

124

under your skirt? A nylon slip? I don't like the feel of nylon, get a silk one instead.' 'What's happened to your nails? I can't bear nails that aren't properly cared for.' The way, on occasion, he would sort of stimulate my acquisitiveness so that he could buy something he wanted and put it down to me. Juliet is wild about Alvar Aalto. Juliet must have her original Breuer chair. (I never sat in the thing, I found it vastly uncomfortable.)

Then something I had noticed: his lightning shunting to the sidelines of anything he couldn't understand, couldn't completely fathom. That's not an important point, that's trivial, don't waste time on it. That's all written down in *Das Kapital* somewhere. Where? I don't know, but it's there, look it up.

'He was a mug like you,' Valeria said. 'More of a mug because he died for it. For this . . .' She faltered and I had the impression that, unusual for her, she was trying to tone down her language, find a gentler term than the one that came first into her mind. 'For this nonsense, this . . . chicken feed. People can only be equal if you force them to it, and forcing them is terrible – it crushes them like beetles. In Budapest we couldn't even paint our houses to make them look nice. Our neighbours did, and then an order came through to hand it over to one of the Party big shots who'd taken a fancy to it.'

'That's not equality, that's another form of domination.'

'No, but it's what you get if you try for it. It's what happens. I've seen it. Ooof,' she made the waving gesture again, 'don't let's talk about this, it only makes me sad. Tell me more about Lorenzo, what did he look like, what was he like with your kid? You're lucky to have a kid, I wish I had one. Only Marcello . . . he's so darn careful he practically carries a puncture kit . . .'

I told her more – almost everything that came into my

mind. *As* it came into my mind: unchecked, uncensored, the way you are supposed to talk to shrinks. His beautiful eyelashes, his hard thin body, his manners that went on being good even when he tried, on ideological grounds, to do without them. The fights with Elvira that went beyond the bounds of manners, into Pinter-land, Chekhov-land. Why do I fall for it, Julie? Why do I bother? Why should I care what she thinks – this witch, this Circe, this *arci, arcistronza*? His similar respect-cum-scorn for the priests who had brought him up. His love for Ubaldo, for Montelupo, for the simple people there whom life had treated hard. His complicated passion for Marco, almost like an English father's: going through agonies for him, wanting him to be so perfect he could hardly bear to correct him, and then, when correction had to be imposed, intervening so hard that it shocked them both – father and son. His shame at his riches – at not being able to get rid of them and not really wanting to either. The motor of his guilt, always turning over, propelling him down roads where the other, sunnier side of his nature balked at going.

'*Cristo!*' said Valeria. (A mildish exclamation in Italian, not a blasphemy.) 'What did he wear for underpants? Sandpaper? Brambles?'

I felt a twinge of disloyalty but couldn't help laughing. 'You don't think there's anything to admire, then, in a rich person who really feels for poorer people, who really cares about them and wants to help them?'

Valeria snorted. 'Poor people! I do *not*. Poor people are *exactly* the same as rich people, no? That's what equality means – that they are exactly, exactly the same. Well . . .'

I started to say something about rights and opportunities, in order to correct this rather simple view of equality, but it sounded pedantic, so I stopped.

'Well, then they are dreadful and that's all there is to it.

Rich people are dreadful – avid, grasping, domineering and all the rest; poor people are just the same as rich people; therefore poor people are avid and grasping and domineering and all the rest. And if they aren't, it's just, like you were saying, because they haven't yet had the opportunity.' She smiled a very sweet smile to counteract the harshness of this view. 'You can love people, I suppose,' she amended. 'All people – if you're Saint Francis or someone. But you can't just love the poor ones. That's weak-headedness.'

Less than a year ago and I would have been at her throat. Or not even, because I probably wouldn't have bothered with a person like Valeria at all. Now her words, raw, naive though they were, struck me as worthy of thinking about and I filed them away in my mind for future attention. Perhaps Lorenzo had indeed had a romantic notion about poverty. Perhaps I had shared it. Was this wrong? Was this weak-headed? A reasoning of a slightly different kind from Valeria's came into my mind: All intellectuals are brainy, and all brainy people are clever, but does it follow from that that all intellectuals are clever? Boh? To borrow di Guido's expression, Boh?

CHAPTER ELEVEN

Last year's summer, coming so close on the horrors, had been an unsettled affair. Most of it spent in the sweltering Roman heat, with Marco and Bice shuttled to and fro to the sea by me, Nicolò, Elvira, whoever had the time.

This year I was determined for Marco's sake to get our lives back on to a proper footing and to spend the hot weather in the relative cool of Montelupo, the way we always had done since he was tiny. Mid June therefore we set off once again, the three of us plus the dog; the car piled high with voluminous holiday items such as pedal cars, tricycles, flippers, and Elvira's imaginative parting gift of a wigwam – fortunately still in its box. I had invited Valeria at the last moment to come with us, but, wisely I think, she had refused. She didn't say so – she never let on that her movements were in any way restricted – but I had the feeling Marcello must have put his foot down. Jealous, probably; frightened of her meeting someone better and taking off.

Things were receding in my mind. My indignation was dying down, the torpor of the judicial system was getting the better of me. Perhaps of everyone. The last meal I'd had with Rita and Piero had been arranged specially to enlist the support of a new journalist friend of theirs who, so they said, had taken Lorenzo's cause deeply to heart, but in fact most of the evening was spent discussing the famous 'butter' scene in Bertolucci's film *Last Tango in Paris*, which the journalist had seen and we hadn't.

My father, much on the same lines, was absorbed by a recently exposed sleaze scandal in the Cabinet. I don't know whether it was genuine interest, in that he knew vaguely some of the people involved, or simply the relief of seeing other well-brought-up English people rolling in the mud, but anyway over the telephone it was hard to get him to talk willingly of anything else.

I took a lot of books with me – non-political, non-anything-in-particular books, just books of mine I'd shelved for ages and now suddenly wanted to read again. Jane Austen. Olivia Manning. Elizabeth Jane Howard. Women writers mostly, and mostly what Lorenzo would have described as 'intimistic', or worse, '*rosa*', meaning pink, for soppy.

Anyway, escapist literature. Yes, if the human heart has an escape valve. So as not to have to worry about bombs and timers and spies and contacts, and lawyers and judges and trials and inquests, and not to have to worry about not worrying about them either.

That was the idea. And that for a while was the reality. Nicolò came and went at intervals, always tightly chaperoned by Elvira. Fine by me. Paolo came for a weekend, too, bringing stacks of papers I could hardly bear to glance through. Rita and Piero came for several. Franny rang chirpily, as if nothing had ever changed between us, and invited herself to stay for Ferragosto – the Italian equivalent of August Bank Holiday – but I knew somehow she would cry off at the last moment, and sure enough she did.

I felt slightly removed from everything, as if I were cocooned in cotton-wool wrappings and life came to me through them – muffled, muted. Even the promptings of my own brain. In the mornings I lay long in the bed that had been the hub of my world with Lorenzo and scarcely thought of him at all. I thought of Mr Darcy instead. And sometimes, to my intense annoyance, of Carosi, whose swarthy face implausibly superimposed itself on that of the blond, slightly languid Darcy of my imagination.

Marco played with the village children, splashed around in the pool and grew brown and picked up an Umbrian accent and slept like a dormouse, and Bice got herself a local boyfriend, a nephew of Cesira's, so in the evenings I was often alone. This suited me better than I'd ever have thought. I would trail my deckchair contentedly along the path of the setting sunrays, moving it every time the shade encroached, and read until the light allowed me. Then I would go into the house and dine off bread and cheese and Ubaldo's vegetables (always the same menu: I felt almost cheated if Cesira cooked something and it changed), read a little more, maybe play patience, and then get ready for bed. When Bice came back – the boyfriend was doing his military service in a nearby barracks, so she, too, was always punctual – I would lock up the house, door after door in the same sequence, and then conk out in a usually dreamless sleep. This tight routine, the first I had observed since childhood, gave me an inexplicable sense of peace. And also of power: rather than marking time I felt as if I was conquering it, forcing it to a standstill.

And thus it happened – very fortunately, all things considered – that I was alone when my peace was shattered and the healing process, that I was vaguely aware of as taking place inside me all this time, was brought to an abrupt halt.

Which shows I might have done better to stick to my routine. But no, for some reason that particular evening I

130

decided to set out the croquet pitch. For the children, I suppose. A new game for Marco and his chums.

It was ages since anyone had played croquet at Montelupo. It was one of the pastimes that, together with the twist and the table-turning, had belonged to an earlier life. The set – a solid and expensive Jacques, specially sent out from England – had been a wedding present from some anglophile cousins of Lorenzo's. I remembered them with great pride announcing it as a 'cricket' set, and myself feeling rather fazed as I thanked them. 'You play cricket a lot in your country, no? It will make you feel very home from home?' Yes, well, not a lot myself, but, er . . . yes, yes, of course.

Our first summer here we had played a good deal – a rough and rumbustious beat-you-to-the-post game that bore the same relation to orthodox croquet as the Grand National to show jumping. For a while it had been fun. Then, when the fun palled, the set had gone back in its box, and the box had been stowed away first in the boiler room, then in the garage, and had finally landed up in the shed at the bottom of the garden where the lawn mower was kept. The way of all trash.

It was there, during a game of hide-and-seek, that I had seen it the day before, wedged behind some spare tiles and things, under Ubaldo's work-bench, and had had the bright idea of fishing it out again.

The light was already fading as I entered the shed and I can't say that I noticed anything unusual from the box's outside appearance. Perhaps there should have been more dust on the top, more cobwebs, seeing how long it had lain untouched, and perhaps it should have been heavier what with the hoops and mallets and all, but it was a quite a struggle to get it out anyway and I honestly didn't notice. The contents were covered by a strip of tarpaulin, a bit of collapsed lilo or part of the undersheet of a tent, and the balls and striped post were lying on top of it, so I didn't notice anything amiss with the inside either, not until I delved deeper in search of the rest. Then, as I began drawing out item after unexpected item, my stomach gradually went hollow, as if someone was siphoning off the air from under my diaphragm, and my heart began hammering in my ears.

Even then, though, my head didn't really register the import of what I had found: it was just my body, getting there first. A dressing-up trunk, that's what I think I imagined at first I had lit upon. With fascinated slowness I lined up the objects and considered them. Two policemen's jackets, badly crumpled, two hats with braid on them. Not policemen's hats exactly, more like airline pilots', but from an unknown airline. A traffic warden's paddle with a stop sign on it. Sticks of greasepaint – dark brown – lots of them, enough for a minstrel band. A pair of heavy rubber gloves, still in their box: German brand, ideal for gardening. An old sweater that was the only thing familiar to me: Lorenzo had used to wear it under his skin-diver's outfit when we stayed with Elvira by the sea and he went underwater fishing. And wrapped inside it a firearm that was so totally unfamiliar I had no idea what it was – whether a rifle or a sub-machine-gun or what – except that it had nothing to do with fishing, underwater or otherwise.

An ache in my jaw brought me out of my trance-like state for a moment and I realized that my mouth was hanging open, literally hanging open, almost to the point of dislocation.

I shut it clumsily with my hand and resumed my search. Books came next – cheap-looking things in Spanish, loads of diagrams showing what looked like electric circuits or the innards of hairdryers or something. Then a pile of –

God, yes, no doubt about this lot, they were passports, and the smaller ones were driving licences – none of them in names that meant anything to me, but all used, and all with the bearer's photograph carefully removed. Then, as the final eye-opener (or jaw-opener: I think my mandible dropped again when I got to this), a little black ball of rolled-up stuff, like a piece of coal in the bottom of the stocking, which when unrolled proved to be – yes, of course, what terrorist kit would be complete without it? – a balaclava helmet.

More of an executioner's mask really. A professional job, well finished off, eye sockets not just cut out but tidily machined and bordered with strips of the same material, cut on the cross. Who made a thing like this, I wondered? What shop could you order it from? Harrods boasted of selling everything – had Lorenzo just rung them up the way he did when he ran out of hankies? 'I need a mask, please. No, not the Zorro variety, a proper one that hides the entire face. Black, adult size. Thank you. Put it down to my wife's account.'

Ubaldo asked me later, shortly before I left, what I felt when the truth struck home to me. I wasn't sure how to answer. To anyone else I'd have said automatically, numbness, shock, but Ubaldo wanted a proper answer and when I mulled it over I decided that shame was the strongest emotion. Shame and a sort of gloating heat that it took me days to classify as what it really was, namely rage at Lorenzo for his betrayal.

I felt so stupid. Wantonly, almost criminally stupid. I didn't know what to do or who to turn to. Still in a kind of trance, or at any rate a bracket state with regard to reality, I pulled the balaclava over my head and went towards the piece of old mirror that Ubaldo kept over the work-bench, beside his *Playboy* calendar, and stared into the glass.

133

'Yours didn't even have eye holes,' I told myself. 'You blind fool, you blind, blind fool.'

Then I went back for the gun and took another look at myself. 'Pampampampam,' I said this time to my reflection. 'Terrorist's moll.' The creature in the mirror laughed mockingly. As well it might.

How long I stood there I don't know, but I know that I suddenly came to my senses and remembered that Marco was alone in the house and that if he woke I wouldn't hear him. (Marco. Another source of anguish there. How was I ever to explain all this to Marco? Oh God, better not to think of it: take one problem at a time.)

Luckily, before I went I had the sense to put everything back the way I had found it and to shove the box into its corner, because the next day was Ubaldo's mowing day and at six he would be already on his mower. He'd have to know soon – everybody would – but to come on the discovery unawares like I had done, I truly think might have given him a stroke.

That night I slept, but only from the small hours onwards. Until Bice came back I sat at the dining-room table laying out patience after patience, a glass of whisky by my elbow which I, who never drink spirits, must have filled at least four times.

I didn't think of anything, not consciously, but my thoughts must have been settling themselves into some kind of order on their own account because as soon as I reached my bedroom (another glass of whisky with me for the night, watered down so as to last) I already knew more or less what I intended to do. I would call Carosi, that was what I would do. I would call him and tell him. Not di Guido, not Elvira, not even Paolo for the time being, but Carosi.

Holding tight to this small capsule of certainty I switched

off the light and lay in the dark, staring at the open window, watching the breeze stir the leaves of the elm tree outside. Some time later I started crying. And some time later still I began to have the first hazy inkling of what I had lost. Not the future this time, but the past: my entire past with Lorenzo, gone in an instant, reduced to a dirty little mound of rubble, as if the bomb had exploded backwards in time, too. When had it started, this double life of his? I would never know. Probably a couple of years back, when he'd begun to do all that travelling, to the north and places, but this would remain a guess. (And the seeds, anyway, must have been there earlier: it wasn't the sort of decision you'd come to overnight – to take up arms against the state in which you lived.) In theory it was possible that he had always been a terrorist, from before I'd even met him, and that all the rest – his doubts, his conversion, the late-night reading sessions, even the rows with Elvira – had been so much eye-wash. Camouflage. Red herrings (what better colour?) to draw us off the scent. There was no way of salvaging any part of our life together; no way of saying, There, up to this moment he and I were one, and then came the rift. The rift was total and permanent and unhealable, and ran from the first day of our meeting onward.

Later still, on the verge of sleep now, I managed to say these things to him more or less direct. Idiot, I told him. Idiot, cretin, liar, Judas. Just look at the shit in which you've landed me. And you couldn't even be a clever terrorist; you had to be a fumbling, bungling, incompetent one. What the blazes was going through your mind all that time? What did you think you'd achieve? We talked about it so often – said what lunatics these people were, how out of touch with reality, how misguided, how wicked even. And all the time you were one of them. A stranger lying here beside me, an alien being, thinking your own thoughts, living your own twisted life; stringing me along; never confiding in me; hiding behind a great thick wall of deceit. Your son thinks you were a hero – I taught him to think of you like that, more fool me. What am I to tell him now? The truth? And how do I tell him that, pray? And when? And what sort of an effect will it have on him?

'I couldn't confide in you, Juliet. Understand that much, I beg of you. I had gone too far in my thoughts for you to follow. But believe me now when I say that what I did, I did in good faith. Because I thought it was the only efficient course of action left.'

Was that what he would have answered? Something of the kind, no doubt. Some unconvincing mixture of lies and claptrap and self-delusion. 'Bite and run.' 'Nothing will go unpunished.' 'Strike one to teach a hundred.' In my halfway state between dreams and consciousness I could see him standing in front of me – a figure out of a child's cartoon, his clothes in tatters, his skin blackened by the blast, holding out his hands imploringly as if in a last attempt at contact before disintegrating altogether. 'Look. Wait. Don't condemn me out of hand. I didn't kill anyone, did I? Only myself. I didn't harm anyone either. Who's to say I ever would have done? All I did was to stash away some gear and fiddle with some explosives I happened to be carrying. The train? The railway line? De-rail the train? Never. I never would have been party to a thing like that. Come on, Juliet, *amore mio*, you know me better than to think . . .'

I didn't know him, not any more. Chances were, I never had done. Chances were I'd never been his *amore* either, merely his brood mare and bed-fellow and a convenient screen for him to hide behind.

'I was never that involved, see. How could I have been? When did I find the time? No, I was just – stupid of me – but I was doing it to help out some friends.'

Nonsense. What friends for a start? Sergio, I bet, the *arcistronzo*. That was why he looked so sick that day in the park. He knew. He was in it, he knew. And he was scared stiff I knew something as well and would babble. Or maybe my first hunch had been right and it was Marta. Or maybe it was both, and maybe Claudia was mixed up in it as well, and Marta's pill of a husband who was always droning away on those wretched Andean pipes or whatever they were called. Maybe they were all in it together. What had Carosi said? It was like a club – someone had to put you up for membership? Well, perhaps they were all members – all except me, the outsider, the wishy-washy Englishwoman with her half-baked notions of democracy who would never understand.

They were bloody well right, I wouldn't.

Then I calmed down a bit and remembered other times, and other Lorenzos surfaced from goodness knows where inside me – my Cambridge pal, my one-time conscience (*conscience?* Yes, he had been that too, incredible to think), my dogged lover, Marco's father – and in their bewildering company I at last must have fallen asleep, because the next thing I knew it was morning, and my mouth tasted like a stale Christmas pudding, and Ubaldo's mower was in full swing on the lawn below.

My heart sank at the thought of Ubaldo. And then rose slightly again: if I could clear that obstacle, I could perhaps clear them all.

CHAPTER TWELVE

In the cold light of morning – well, no, it was baking hot already, but anyway in the hot light of morning my idea of turning to Carosi seemed madness, so I rang Elvira instead and blurted everything out to her there and then, over the telephone. To worry at this stage about the line being tapped struck me as about as senseless as being on the sinking *Titanic* and worrying if your dress was ironed.

She was, thankfully, her best crisis self. 'Don't move, *piccola*, don't do anything. I'm coming straightaway. Don't breathe a word to anyone, *va bene*? Don't touch the box. Get Cesira to make you some nice strong coffee, and then go and drink it the garden and wait for me to arrive. It'll be all right, you'll see. Everything will be all right.'

When she arrived, driven by a studiedly po-faced Marini, she looked almost relieved. And on my account she probably was: it couldn't have been easy, living close to me all this time without ever being able to shake off entirely her suspicions that I was a militant in the so-called Red Brigades. (So-called? Rightly called. Alas, all, all too rightly called.) I could understand that now, just as she could understand things from my point of view. Or so I hoped: logic was never exactly her strong point.

We hugged one another with real pathos, real affection.

Marini stood by, immobile, and looked detached. Had his ears been on hinges, though, I think he'd have swivelled them like a fox's or a radar panel.

'*J'ai dou le porrrter*,' Elvira whispered at me loudly in her heavily accented French. (She held French to be an impenetrable language for employees, and even used it in front of Ubaldo and Cesira who had spent fourteen years in a Belgian mining town and spoke it fluently.) '*Je ne pouvais pas conduirrr dans cette condition.*' And she held out her hands which indeed were shaking like maracas.

We went, not straight but as straight as we could without further arousing Marini's curiosity, down to the shed and bolted ourselves in. In silence I pulled out the incriminating chest and spread everything out again. When I had finished it looked like a stall in the Portobello Road.

'There, that's the lot,' I said. 'What do we do now?'

Elvira made no immediate reply. She startled me by doing much as I had and placing one of the airline berets on her head and going over to the mirror to inspect herself. As she raised her hand something fluttered out of the hat – a price-tag or a piece of paper – but I was too intent on watching her to follow its flight, and when I looked again it was gone.

'Hideous!' she said after a moment, hurling the hat to the ground. '*Brutto, brutissimo!*' With such passion in her voice that I knew she was really referring to the situation. Then her eyes filled with tears and she groped around her for somewhere to sit, ending up eventually on the seat of the mower and staining her beautiful cream silk skirt with grass. 'What do we do? What *can* we do? We have no choice really, do we?'

A pause after the 'really' told me she was thinking something I had hardly dared think of myself, but that nevertheless in some form or other must have been lurking in my mind as I had no trouble grasping her meaning. 'You mean we . . . ?' And with my fingertips I made the minia-ture gesture of closing the chest and stowing it away again under the work-bench.

Elvira moved her head faintly; you could scarcely call it a nod.

We looked at one another hard and both of us gave a tiny guilty smile. A pin, no, but a dropped nail you could have heard, maybe even a tin-tack. I had never felt her so close or so available. If I said yes, she would be mine for ever. She would love me – she would have to; she would be the mother I had missed out on, she would be a prop and an ally and a friend for life.

And what would our silence matter? This stuff had been in the box for over a year now: as clue material it was cold as ice. The police would probably go and lose it anyway, they seemed to specialize in that. We could burn it – apart from the buttons on the uniform it'd all burn like fun. We could drag it out tonight, in the dead of night like the conspirators it would make us, and dump it all in Ubaldo's rubbish pit and pour petrol on it and hop round the flames while it burned. Elvira wouldn't have a terrorist son to explain away to her shame to the rest of the family, I wouldn't have a terrorist husband, Marco wouldn't have a terrorist father. The judges would be spared the extra work. And – no small consideration either – the police wouldn't come galumphing in again to rip up another stretch of floor and bash more holes in the walls.

This was what I thought, and what I prepared myself to say, but the words came out differently. 'Who do we call first? *Carabinieri* or di Guido?' was what I actually said.

Elvira shot me a look so complicated I don't know what was in it, whether resentment or admiration or gratitude or despair or a bit of all. 'This is what you've wanted all along, isn't it, Giulietta?' She began in a knife-edged voice but then, to her credit, covered her mouth in horror and begged me to forget she'd ever spoken.

'No, you're right,' she went on in a completely different tone – tired, kind, much older-sounding. 'You're so right. We can't. We couldn't have. It would have been a dreadful mistake. And it's too late anyway.'

My thoughts went to the telephone call I'd made to her, and I started rather lamely to apologize – what on earth was there to apologize for on my side? – but she interrupted me quickly.

'No it's not that, it's Marini. He's picked up something, didn't you notice? When I rang him – well, I was so distraught, I don't know what I said. Nothing definite, I don't think, but I may just . . . without meaning to . . . just have let slip something about the chest. Nothing about the contents, I'm sure, but . . . *O merda!*' She got up and began pacing the shed, glancing nervously out of the window as she passed: guilt seemed to scatter off this affair like pollen. *Merda* sounded so weird on Elvira's lips it almost made me laugh. 'Anyway,' she went on, raking dramatically at her hair, which remained perfect as before, 'I could hear that layabout son of his in the background, making comments and asking questions, and I wouldn't be at all surprised if he has already alerted the press. He wanted to cadge a lift with us – imagine – said he had business in Perugia. Business, if you please! From what I know he's never lifted a finger in his life.'

This gave me a proper fright. If the news got out before we gave it out, it would look as if we'd been trying to hide things. As if *I* had anyway. Which to some extent was true: strictly speaking I suppose I should've reported my find the evening before, not waited until now.

Elvira, in the annoyingly passive way she sometimes adopted just when action was called for, insisted we did nothing until we had taken counsel from our respective lawyers.

I gave in, because it seemed quicker than arguing and by now my fear was close to panic, but thankfully neither Paolo nor Russo could be found, so in the end we settled for di Guido. And again told him everything, over the phone – the exact time of discovery, the list of the objects, the lot.

Within less than an hour the police were with us: two carloads, they must have come from Perugia to have arrived so soon. Sirens, flashing lights, grim-faced uniformed men swarming all over the place like paratroopers on a raid. Half an hour later another van rolled up and a further group emerged in plain clothes – members of a special anti-terrorist squad, as they qualified themselves later – and immediately, like in the movies, began quarrelling with their colleagues on the spot over methods of procedure.

The leader of this second onslaught, a youngish man with the most rampant case of pyorrhoea I had ever seen, treated me from the start with a loathing so stark as to result in the end in being merely unprofessional. Maybe it was the combination of swimming pool and sedition, or the fact that, me having called him in and not vice versa, he couldn't arrest me as he was clearly longing to, but anyway he added significantly to the miseries of that already miserable day.

As it did in the other moments of high drama – the bomb night, the funeral, particularly the funeral – my memory seems to have carried out a kind of stew-pot operation. The flavour of the whole is pretty well uniform, and uniformly nasty, but the bits that have kept their character are not necessarily either the worst or the most important, just the ones that for some reason or other happen to have stuck in my head. I am sure, for example, that the man with pyorrhoea must have questioned me closely, because I can see the red rim of his gums going on and off like a neon strip, appearing and disappearing as the lips part in speech and then again close, but I can't seem to remember any of his questions or any of my answers.

It's like my fascination for the spittle on the telephone the night of the explosion; it's absurd. Although I remember clearly him denying me permission at one point to go upstairs in answer to Bice's summons and have a look at Marco's heat rash – mainly I think because he was so rude about it. 'Let the other woman go,' he said, pointing at Elvira, 'the grandmother.' At which Elvira, who hated being classified as a grandmother, turned on him and said loftily that she had no experience of children's ailments, *grazie tanto*, always having been able to rely on the help of fully qualified nurses. I loved her for this, but it didn't improve the atmosphere.

What he must have been getting at, I suppose, or trying to get at, was more information about the stuff in the box. Who it was meant for, where it had come from, whether it had been used in some past action or was waiting to be used in the future. Things about which I had no more knowledge than he did, in fact probably a great deal less. Had I noticed how carefully the clothes were folded? Did he ask me that? Yes, I think he must have done. And other things, too, like why had I pulled the contents out in the first place, and why had I put them back again and then pulled them out a second time – was I aware it might look like a deliberate attempt to confuse? And was the shed kept locked? And who had the key? And had anyone over the past year tried to gain access to either?

These questions, yes, I infer rather than recall directly. Ubaldo was interrogated later that day, by the same horrid man, and according to him these were the points he harped on most: keys, access, suspect people hanging around the property or trying to break in. It stands to reason really: as a policeman it was the future he was interested in, not the past; the living terrorists, not the dead ones. The only other words of his that I remember verbatim – for their surprise value, which was considerable once I had worked out the meaning – came at the end of the session, when di Guido arrived and mercifully put an end to my torment by taking over the questioning himself. 'Oh ho,' the man said as he rose to make place for the judge, a sneer in his voice heavier than the one he had reserved for Elvira. 'Oh ho. The Signora really does have some *santi in paradiso*, and no mistake: for months we're not allowed to go near her – we are assured on the highest authority she knows nothing; and now, when she certainly does know something, or ought to, we're not allowed to speak to her. I wish I had her connections, I truly do.'

Someone, some high-placed contact of Elvira's probably, had been keeping the anti-terrorist squad off my back.

The police concentrated their activities on the shed this time round and left the masonry mercifully untouched, but all the same it was late afternoon by the time they finished their overhaul and left us in peace. Marco loved watching them at work: unlike the rest of us he had a great day. The last thing they did was to carry out the croquet box and load it into their van, and what with the shape of the thing and the way they handled it it was just like a second funeral.

Ubaldo had been hanging round since morning, unwilling to leave his precious tools unguarded, and as the box passed in front of us I turned to him and hid my face in the sleeve of his hunting shirt so as not to see. He gave a hiss of disapproval at the bearers, *Schiih!* like an angry snake, and hugged me to him tight. So far he had made no comment, either on the find, or on what it meant, as if Lorenzo's betrayal had literally left him speechless. Now, as the van drew away, he prised my chin up with one of his rough

144

miner's fingers and looked me straight in the face and I saw that his eyes, like mine, were full of tears. Although strangely the expression was not entirely sad. 'I thought it was you they'd come for, Giulietta,' he said. 'God forgive me, when I got here this morning and saw all the commotion I thought it was you.'

'I'm glad it wasn't,' was all I could think of replying. Lorenzo had always claimed all Ubaldo's love for himself, saying that I only came in for loyalty in my position as wife. But now I realized that some of it must have brushed off on to me as well, and I felt a huge surge of pride, as if I had made a great and difficult conquest.

'So am I,' Ubaldo said. 'Lorenzo I can deal with – I'll have to deal with it, won't I? – but you, no, I couldn't have taken that. Not that.'

CHAPTER THIRTEEN

That night Elvira stayed on, and we sat up late, sousing ourselves silly with some horrible walnut liqueur, which was all the alcohol I could find now that I'd polished off the whisky.

Lorenzo disliked spirits even more than I did, and I think I must have done it in order to spite him, in order to have something tangible to reproach him with. Look what you've done to me, look what you've brought me to – your wife, turning into a drunkard. In the same perverse spirit I went through almost half a packet of cigarettes as well, drawing the smoke deep into my lungs and relishing the rasp as it went.

The conversation lagged – mainly because we were talking about different things: me about the inside of Lorenzo's head, that I had failed so abysmally to penetrate, and Elvira chiefly about the outside of her own. How could she face her sister Serena now, who had always criticized her for the way she brought up her sons? Would I tell her that, please, would I tell her? How could she ever again spend Easter in the family get-together in the Argentario? How could she go around in any society worth keeping, with everyone knowing the monster that had come out of her womb? The presidential receptions of the past – for

Marshall Tito, for Haile Selassie – when again would she ever be invited to one of those? It was finished; her life in Roman society was over.

'Oh, come on, Elvira. Presidential receptions. You never did go anyway.'

'Of course not. But I like to be invited. Nobody will invite me now, nobody. I can hardly bear to look at myself, I shall have to shroud all the mirrors like the Contessa di Castiglione.'

And on and on. Wail, wail, worse than Cassandra. Occasionally branching off from her centre theme to deliver dire social predictions for me and Nicolò and Marco as well.

Around midnight, having run out of laments, she took herself off to bed. But my mind was still chasing vainly after Lorenzo's, and instead of following her I went into the little upstairs sitting room that he had used as a study and began pulling books off the shelves and riffling through them. Much as the *carabinieri* had done in their first blitz.

In search of what? To begin with I wasn't sure, but as the feeling of drunkenness died down I felt another replace it – that fiery, almost gleeful sensation that had come over me in the shed: the lust of the hunter, the avenger – and I realized that what I was after was not so much an insight into Lorenzo's thoughts as further confirmation of his falseness. How deep was his betrayal? When had it started? And what had sparked it off?

I had little material to go on. Only books: notes and papers had been removed at the time of the first search, and more stuff – atlases, I think, and a big scientific dictionary – had gone today. No good telling them it was mine, used only for plant names.

I followed the grime first, the grime that goes with heavy thumbing. And within the grimy bits I sought ear-marks and underlinings. I had done most of my duty reading in English, so I knew these traces were Lorenzo's.

For a while I floundered, unable to discern any meaningful pattern, but gradually little overall bits of information began to emerge. For example, every single book had been read in the same way: the first ten pages or so thoroughly, the next ten merely skimmed, and the rest – virtually untouched, unopened. Some texts, particularly from the university presses, had the old-fashioned cut-as-you-go pages, and in these the habit was still more evident: a couple of chapters slit, and the remainder sealed as tight as on the day of purchase.

The underlining, too, had the same rhythm to it – quite irrespective of content, or so it seemed. On the opening page nearly all the text heavily underscored, and then a constant falling off and thinning out – every other line, every other two, other three, other four – until, round about page 20 or so, the marks petered out altogether. It was crazy, I had to go back several times and check before I could believe it.

Lenin – State and Revolution. Fifty pages of bland, balancing-act introduction on the part of some highly cautious Italian intellectual, of which the first fifth was peppered literally black with stress marks. What on earth was the point? Then Lenin's own short preface, with the opening sentence underlined also: 'The problem of the state takes on a particular importance today, both from the theoretical viewpoint and the practical political one.' Again, what was the point? What on earth, on earth, on earth was the point? Nothing remarkable in those words that I could see, except for the stunning banality they expressed. Then the text itself – clean as driven snow, with the spine of the book still cracking as I opened the pages.

Einaudi's edition of Che Guevara's speeches. Same thing

more or less, only in this case the editor's foreword was so short that some of the original text came in for a bit of pencilling as well. 'I met him (Castro, of course, it was all about Castro) on one of those cold Mexican nights, and I remember that our first conversation was about the problems of international politics.' Could that really deserve an underlining? Eh, Che Gherardi? Eh? With your resemblance to the author, wouldn't you have done better to cut the photograph off the cover and stick it into one of your phoney passports? Eh?

Gramsci – *Letters from Prison*. I'd never been able to make head or tail of Gramsci, even when my head was clear, but no matter: here, too, were the same set of spoors in the same distribution: marks as thick as wickerwork at the outset, and then dwindle dwindle and then stop.

The clinch however came with Volume I of Marx's *Kapital*. I knew my way round that a little. More than a little: I had waded through it with my mental galoshes on; I had thought at the time that Lorenzo and I had waded through it together, side by side in our puritanical bedtime study sessions. Value theory. Surplus-value. Historical materialism. The dialectic method – those childish drawings we made (at least *I* did) of three-pronged springs, to try and din it into our heads what was meant by it and how it worked. All that slogging, all that pondering – and where had Lorenzo been while it was going on? Still on Marx's analysis of the cost of linen coats by the looks of things. It was not possible.

And yet it was. Look it up, Julie. Where? I don't know where. Stop plaguing me with all your questions and find out for yourself. Don't read if you can't understand. Go back to your Brontës.

But that was what I was reading these books *for*: in order to understand. What was he reading for? For catchwords?

For a glazing of knowledge just deep enough to kid other people? Or to kid himself?

The very last word he had underlined – twice, and in red biro – was 'fetishism'. It had stood him in good stead. 'Bourgeois fetishists', 'the fetishes of the consumer society', 'property nothing but a fetish'. The link between wealth and something vaguely kinky, smutty: it had gone down very well at the student rallies. No good pointing out to him, as I tried to once, that Marx used a wooden table as a typical example of a fetish, and that, since tables weren't exactly a middle-class prerogative (though a Breuer chair, yes?), perhaps Marx had had a wider meaning of the term in mind.

'Don't quibble, Juliet. You're worse than a Byzantine theologian.' Hardly surprising in the end that he preferred pillow fights to arguments.

Exhausted by now, and aware of being so, I banged the books to with vehemence and clapped them back on shelves, as if they were living things that I could punish. Only *Kapital* I kept with me, with a vague idea of re-reading.

As I got into bed I could hear the telephone downstairs ringing and ringing, and Elvria's voice shouting out to me to answer it. I shouted back that it would only be more journalists and that I was taking the wretched thing off the hook.

From her room came a noise like a banshee, 'Please, Giulietta. *Ti supplico!* It might be Nicolò.' Nicolò, lucky him, was sailing round the Greek islands with friends, opportunely out of reach. 'Something might have happened to him – there may have been another *disgrazia*. Quick!'

If she was that worried then why didn't she go herself? Rather crossly I thumped downstairs again in the dark, muttering more accusations against Lorenzo who said two telephones in the country would be an insult to the locals who often didn't even have one, and lifted the receiver.

It wasn't Nicolò and it wasn't the press; it was, of all people, Carosi.

A very faraway voice: he was calling from Norway, where he was on holiday, and was full of apologies for the lateness of the hour, but the news had only just reached him through a colleague. Was I all right? Was di Guido there to take care of things? Were the anti-terrorist people causing difficulties? Was there anything he himself could do to help?

From Norway? In the middle of the night? He could bask in the midnight sunshine and give another smirk of satisfaction, that's what. Although to do him justice his voice seemed genuinely concerned. In fact there was a hesitancy in it that, had I not known him better, I would have put down to shyness.

'I will be back in the first week of September, Signora Gherardi. I presume you are not staying on in the country? We could meet then in Rome, in my office. Let's say nine-thirty on the Wednesday morning.'

If we had to. Up to him. I made some rather graceless reply to this effect and replaced the receiver without giving him time to add more.

Afterwards, however, I remembered my strange decision of yesterday evening to contact him, and how compelling it had seemed then, and I regretted my haste.

'Who was it?' Elvira called out as I reached the landing.

'Nobody,' I said, slightly to my own surprise. 'Nobody important.'

CHAPTER FOURTEEN

This is the second summer you have loused up for me, I told
Lorenzo in a fury, as I closed the shutters on a still brilliant
sun and prepared to return to Rome and to my meeting
with Carosi.

Elvira had stayed another week, shielding me (the verb
was hers) from the backlash of this second scandal. She
disapproved of Marco's friends, she disapproved of Bice's
boyfriend, she said terrible things in terrible French about
Cesira's cooking – I honestly would have preferred the
hounding of the press.

Who in fact hardly bothered us at all. Watergate and a
cholera outbreak in Naples had far more news value than a
pile of old clothes in a trunk, and the Italian August is a
holiday month for journalists, too, along with everyone
else. We got a fair number of telephone calls, but only two
reporters thought it worth their while to make the climb to
Montelupo in the flesh, and both were soon deflected by the
heat and the erratic firing habits of the local *cacciatori*,
practising for the autumn slaughter. A brace or two of
humans in their bag on the opening day being quite a
routine occurrence.

Relatives, sympathetic and not, proved far more trouble,
as Elvira had foreseen. Calls poured in from the various

152

aunts and uncles advising – in some cases threatening – flight, changes of surname, emigration to South America, all sorts of consoling tactics. And my poor lawyer Paolo was so shattered that I spent the entire afternoon of his visit ministering to him, and not vice versa. Until now, in the face of growing evidence to the contrary, he had stuck to his opinion that all terrorism was black. When it masked itself in red, it was due to the Machiavellian deviousness of the secret services, intent on ruining the image of the Communist Party, but underneath, you could still bet on it, it was black as pitch, fascist as the dastardly old Duce himself.

Now, having come slap up against a real red terrorist, if only a dead one, he was thrown into confusion. The colours of his whole political spectrum ran awash. The few left-wing thinkers so far who had dared voice this awkward opinion of the 'opposti estremismi' – two opposite types of extremism, that is, springing from the Left and the Right – had been shouted down and accused of heresy: now it seemed that he had no choice but to join the heretics. 'What goes through the heads of people like your husband, Giulietta, that's what I can't understand?' He repeated time after time, drumming his fists against his skull as if the answer could somehow be got at by splitting open his own. 'What goes through their daft, mushy, lunatic heads? Don't they realize they're playing right into the fascists' hands? You know, if I met one of them I don't think I'd even turn them in, I'd just take them to a cave or somewhere and tie them up, and then say, Now, tell me what in the name of Carlo maledetto Marx you think you're doing? I'd take them food every day, I'd listen to them for as long as it took to tell me, but I'd just have to try and get them to make me understand.'

No one could know better than I what he meant. It was a dialogue I was engaged in in my head with Lorenzo all the time. Only my words were angrier. What the fucking, fucking hell did you think you were doing, you pampered, doctrinaire guerrilla of the eleventh hour? What the fucking, fucking hell did you hope to achieve? Guns, explosives – who were they meant for? Innocent passers-by, like that poor young girl in Milan Central Police Station who only went there to get her passport renewed? Messengers, couriers, like the man in Genoa who was shot because he wouldn't hand over the pay packets? Twenty-year-old *carabinieri*, like the ones blown up by the car bomb in the north? Sons of Ubaldo, gone into the force from poverty and an old-fashioned notion of rectitude and public service? Are those the enemy, the people you want to eliminate? Tell me, for goodness sake. Explain, give me some kind of reason or I think I shall do my nut trying to find one.

If I had been sure about Sergio's involvement and had known how to broach the subject with him, I think I would have sought him out and put these questions to him. Anything to get an insight. But was I sure? Not entirely. I suspected, that was all. I strongly, strongly suspected.

And then, if my suspicion was right, what would I do? Denounce him? And what would he do? Sit around calmly and wait to be denounced? Or would he . . . ?

Would he what? Try to stop me? And if so, how? 'For your own safety,' Carosi had said. No, to approach the *arcistronzo*, whether he was involved or not, was unthinkable.

I was still engaged in this kind of vacillating monologue as I locked the front door and put the key in its hiding place in the wall, ready for Cesira to pick up the next day, Monday, when she came to clean.

I meant what I said about the lousing up of my summer. I hated leaving Montelupo at this time, in this weather. September was the most precious month of all, and it was the last at our disposal for a long time. Next year Marco would have to go to school, and new directives from the Ministry of Education had recently put forward the opening date of all schools, public and private, to the first week of September. A measure that for once found me absolutely in agreement with Elvira: all this talk of modernity and keeping pace with Europe; *so* much better in her day, when she and the children had been able to linger on by the sea until halfway through October.

As I walked towards the car, thinking these things and grumbling to myself about them in my head, I had a sudden itchy feeling that I had forgotten something, left some essential part of the closing procedure unfinished, so I called out to Bice to get out of the car and go and sit in the shade with Marco and the dog while I made a check.

It took me two unfruitful tours of the house, inside and out, before I realized what it was that was bothering me. The toolshed, that was it, there was some suspended business connected with the toolshed, although precisely what, I couldn't say for sure unless I was on the spot.

I walked there slowly, fingering the keys and trying to remember which it was that opened the shed and whether Ubaldo had ever shown me or even left me a duplicate, and as I walked the missing detail came back to me. With the rhythm of a slow-motion film I saw Elvira's raised hand as she tried on the beret in front of the mirror, and then, flippity, flippity, that little patch of white as the label or whatever it was crossed my field of vision to disappear I knew not where in the region behind the work-bench.

I must retrieve it. Find out what it was. Take it if necessary to di Guido or even the man with the disastrous gums.

Should it, that is, prove important. But even before I opened the door and went to the bench and rocked it forward a little and started probing into the sawdusty compost that had accumulated behind, I knew somehow that it would turn out to be important. Probably, I don't know, I had seen more than just the flash of white: I don't really believe in hunches and intuitions.

When at last I found it and fished it out I saw it was a photograph. A polaroid snap, showing the face of a largish tenement building – beehivey, modern, fairly anonymous. The walls were of a muddy grey colour, slightly warmer than dun, and the ironwork of the balconies was picked out in black. Had it not been for the coloured splashes afforded by the washing hung out on some of the balconies to dry, it might have passed almost for a black-and-white photograph. And had it not been for the detail of a birdcage hanging outside the window of one of the apartments it might not even have caught my attention. I might just have crumpled the thing up and thrown it away.

Instead I pocketed it, promising myself I would deliver it to the police as soon as I got back, and for the whole of the homeward drive tinkered with the sluggish machinery of my memory, trying to get it to spark. I had seen that birdcage. I had seen the bird inside – a nondescript little brown songbird I couldn't put a name to, hopping dolefully from bar to bar – and I had been sorry for it. I had watched it moreover for quite a longish stretch of time. Not heard it, no, I was too far away for that, but I had watched and watched while some other sound filled my ears. A twangy voice. On tape. Donovan or Cat Stevens. Yes, Cat Stevens, I think. I had watched from behind the car windscreen, therefore, waiting while Lorenzo conducted one of his business meetings inside the building. (Business meetings? I suppose you could call them that.) But when? Where? In what city? In what street?

Try as I might I could get no further response. I had waited outside so many buildings, on so many occasions.

156

Often I read, sometimes I just closed my eyes and dozed. It was the purest fluke this particular wait had left the mark it had done, but the date, the location, the address . . . hopeless.

By the time we reached Rome I had changed my mind about handing the snapshot over to the police – it would be of scant use to them anyway unless I could furnish more details – and had decided to give it straight to Carosi instead, whom I was due to see on the very next day. I rang his number to tell him this, but there was no reply. Then I started on the dreary task of unpacking, stowing away the summer with the bathing suits, saluting for another year my country freedom. The dog, Leonessa, watched, and panted, and agreed.

It was when evening had already fallen, and I was in the shower, humming a tune to myself that only later I identi-fied as the one I had listened to that day in the car, that the answer came to me. Too late, or so I tried to convince myself, to notify anyone. It was Rome. Definitely. Rome – north of the city, not far from where I was now. A newly built residential area on the fringes of the countryside. Besides the poor little caged bird I had seen sheep, grazing in the open on the far side of the building. I could remember that clearly now, remember how I had contrasted the plights of the two kinds of creatures – freedom and im-prisonment – and thought how they sort of went together in this lackadaisical country that was Italy. No caged song-birds in London flats, but no meandering sheep in the vicinity either, watched over by a shepherd who, barring the jeans, might have come straight out of Virgil.

It had been hot in the car that day. I had been thirsty, and at one point had got out and looked around for a shop or a café. I hadn't found one and hadn't really bothered to try, but nevertheless that brief scan had left an imprint, if only I

157

could freshen it up. A square, that was where the car had been parked, a little square with a paper stall set right in the centre. A paper stall and a flower seller in a glass kiosk. Back to back, like Siamese twins. An advertisement hoarding on the far side of the square that dwarfed both. Some kind of water fount – I recalled the impression of coolness, hadn't however dared drink the water: a fountain, or a trough. A few sad little urban trees, heavily pruned, no shadow. Acacia? Robinia? Perhaps, only Judas trees was more likely: they were the ones who came in for the worst cropping as a rule. Judas – very fitting. Could I find the place on such information? I thought I could.

Whether I should was another matter, but I didn't dwell long on this: my hunting spirit was up again. I made another go at Carosi's number, just so as I could tell him honestly that I'd tried, waited to the count of twelve while it rang unanswered, and then told Bice I was going out and not to stay up for me.

The light was failing but even so the search didn't take me long: the area was new, raw, unfinished, the way I remembered it. Few public spaces, fewer amenities; what Piero and Rita's architect friends would have called a dormitory quarter. All I had to do was to drive there, ask passersby to direct me to a newsagent's, and on my second try, there it was – the stall in the middle of the square, the flower kiosk, shuttered for the night, and the tall grey tenement block of the photograph on the left-hand side, its windows glowing feebly here and there in the darkness. Telly viewers. Mosquito zone. Well-to-do inhabitants, most of them still summering by the sea. Too dark now to see the bird.

As yet I had just acted on impulse. I had no plan in my head of what I would do when I found the place, or if indeed I would do anything. Bar look perhaps: sit there in the car in the same passive fashion I had done before, and

158

look. Watch. See who came out, who went in. Now I was on the spot however my curiosity became feverish, impossible to suppress. How many flats were there on this side of the building? Round about a dozen by the looks of things, assuming there were two per storey; more if they were smaller. How could I tell which was the one Lorenzo had visited? Presumably it was the one which figured most centrally in the photo, but like a fool I hadn't brought the photo. All the same, the photographer, whoever he was, had definitely concentrated on the middle slice, so I could pretty safely rule out the ground floor and the top, which left me with the four in-betweeners. Eight, or possibly twelve, different apartments. Of which – let's see – only four showed signs of life going on inside.

Four, that wasn't bad. (Bad in what sense? What was I intending to do if I identified the hide-out? I still hadn't thought this out. Cunning of me in a way, or else I'd have been obliged to stop: part of me must have already known I was doing something rash and wrong that could land me in a mass of difficulties later.) What if I got out of the car and looked at the names on the intercom? Could I whittle the number down further?

Guilt and curiosity were so mixed up in me now that, rather like dogs do when they're torn by two instincts and suddenly chuck both and give themselves over to frantic scratching, all I felt was the overriding desire to act. To move, to do something, no matter what. I got out of the car and went to the doorway, where the names of the various inhabitants were listed on a dully lit plaque, each name flanked by a corresponding number and button, and started counting.

Twenty-ruddy-eight, if you please. Twenty-eight different dwellings. The figure was so much higher than I had reckoned on that I had a moment's despair. No way either of telling whether the numbers went according to lay-out, and whether they started at the top and went downwards, or vice versa, or neither.

Mechanically, almost randomly, I started pressing buttons. There were very few replies. Someone with an old man's wheeze shouted tetchily several times, '*Chi è, perdinci?*' before slamming the receiver down. Someone else said, '*Maria?*' and then added an insult. A third person just said, '*Vieni su,*' Come on up, and buzzed open the front door for me. Some other more personal kind of suspicion must have been lying dormant in me for a long time however for I was struck immediately by the tone of the last answer to reach me. A girl's voice – young, fresh, sleepy-sounding – just said a querying, '*Si?*' Nothing more than that – the one soft monosyllable – and a ripple went through me like a low-volt electric shock.

'*Si?*' said the voice again. Quick, which button did it belong to, which name? This one: Certaldo, apartment 7B.

I took a fast deep breath as I made up my mind. 'I'm a friend of Lorenzo's,' I said. There was no need to feign drama, I was keyed to the nines. 'I need to see you, I need help.'

There was silence from the mouthpiece. A live silence. Followed by a slightly bewildered Oh, and what sounded like a whispered consultation with another person in the background.

Advice must have been forthcoming as the voice spoke again, but by that time I was heading towards the opened door and heard only the sound, not the words. I knew I must take advantage of the surprise factor: if I'd got the right place, and these people really were the terrorists I was looking for, they'd only let me in if I was quick, gave them no proper thinking time.

The hall branched off into two separate trunks, leading

presumably to different staircases, different lifts. A's on the left, B's on the right? No, I thought I'd seen C's and D's on the intercom as well. (Why the hell hadn't I checked this before moving? Stupid nit.) A's and B's on the left, therefore; then, if my guess was right, there should be another division.

There was. A short corridor, then another hall and two staircases. I took the right-hand one this time and ran up four flights without pausing. There were two doors on the landing, neither of which bore the name Certaldo, but as I stood there debating which one to try I saw a thin shaft of light coming from the floor below and ran down again – almost slid – just in time to catch the sound of the click as the door to one of the apartments shut to.

There was no Certaldo here either. A small printed card was nailed underneath the doorbell saying: 'Combi-plan S.r.l.', or some other name like that with which the Italian business world abounds. Nevertheless I pressed my hand on the bell outside and kept it there, and sure enough, after only the briefest wait I found myself looking into a pair of eyes that I seemed already to have encountered, so perfectly did they match the voice I had heard over the machine.

CHAPTER FIFTEEN

What is it about sexual jealousy? What is it about the attraction that accompanies it – that strange rasping pull that crosses the borders of gender so that we are drawn despite ourselves to the partners of our partners? How did I know for certain the moment I saw the girl that she had been Lorenzo's lover?

Because I felt myself in unwilling sympathy with her, that's why. Because I liked the look of her short fluffy hair and her elfin ears sticking through it, and the full wavy mouth that seemed to belong to some other face, far more sensual, and the thin graceful limbs adroop with fatigue and yet tense, poised, ready to start into motion at the first hint of aggression on my part. I suppose they all lived like that, these people, on the brink of fear round the clock, and I suppose that was part of the charm of their addlepated lives. Security was the great bourgeois treasure, and they had forfeited it, scorned it as dross. The last word in snobbery, if you think the matter through.

The only flaw in this theory of recognition is that the appeal should presumably have worked both ways, whereas it palpably didn't. The girl's curlicue mouth fell open when she saw me and then dipped downwards at the corners like a clown's. 'But you're the wife,' she said in dismay. 'You're his wife, you're Hosay's wife.'

Hosay? What was that? Oh, I see: José: Lorenzo's battle name. How could he have let himself be called José and kept a straight face? I could hardly keep one myself. José, Simon, Emilio, Pancho. But it wasn't funny, nothing in the situation was funny. The knowledge of this ulterior, physical, betrayal went through me like a skewer and lodged somewhere inside me: quite painless as yet but threatening pain in future. It was there, it would fester, it would stab into me with every move I made. Italian women looked on their husband's carnal escapades with benign acceptance, almost pride – when I asked Bice if she was ever worried about her *fidanzato* fooling around with other women she laughed and said, 'Why? It doesn't wear out with use, does it? As long as I'm the only one he marries.' But I knew with me it would be different: I would take it the way the men did, as a dishonour, a belittlement.

The girl looked every bit as shaken by our encounter as I was myself. I am not photogenic, perhaps she had imagined me uglier, dowdier, easier to dismiss. 'Why have you come here?' she said with a shiver. I noticed she made no attempt to close the door or prevent my entry. 'What is it you want?'

I shrugged so as not to seem too eager to get inside. I wasn't eager, either, now I came to think of it, I didn't care a fig any more: I had already found out more than I cared to know, and serve me right.

'Well,' she said, scanning the stairs behind me nervously, 'make up your mind. If you want to come in you can come in, if not . . .'

I went in, touching her arm by mistake as I went past and then shying away as if disgusted by the contact. She felt clean and warm and healthy, and I wasn't really disgusted at all. On the contrary I was perversely intrigued. Had she

163

and Lorenzo made love that day, I wondered, while I sat downstairs in the car, safely plugged into my tape recorder? Oh God, please no, I couldn't bear to see myself in the role of dim-witted, unsuspecting spouse.

The apartment was tidy, well kept, well furnished in a rather flashy kind of way: it didn't look like a terrorists' den in any respect. There was a chandelier, a pair of glossy wooden bookshelves – slightly bare of volumes, to tell the truth – a glass coffee table set with books and ashtrays, a carpet, a low leather sofa with matching armchairs, and a telly with a wedding photograph prominently displayed on the top. The home of a nice young professional couple, newlyweds, without children.

And without imagination. For a moment my heart lightened: the man in the photograph, although familiar to me in a vague sort of way, was not Lorenzo, and the décor, now I came to observe it closer, was of a banality such as would have set my egalitarian husband's teeth on edge, no matter how sexy he had found the lady of the house: lace curtains, heart-shaped cushions, even a gilt-edged recess in the wall housing a row of porcelain dolls dressed as choir-boys.

Then I realized my foolishness. And my own banality. This was a *real* terrorists' hide-out. Perhaps not an operative one, or whatever the term was for the place they faked their passports and held their captives and cooked up their explosives and whatnot, but a real habitation, affording living space and storage and cover to real flesh-and-blood terrorists. Above all, cover. I'd bet there were no frills and laces inside the cupboards. (Unless, that is, they were as fussy as Luchino Visconti was reputed to be about his film sets, which I doubted.) I'd bet if you opened the fridge or the dresser or the bedside drawers you'd find it was a different story: chloroform, gags, knuckle-dusters, couple of Kalashnikovs, the odd amputated ear lobe – dainty little knick-knacks like that.

There was no sign of the other person I'd heard the girl consulting with over the intercom, but I could feel that he or she was there, concealed and listening. Not that this bothered me much either. After all I was José's widow – *la viuda de José* – and warped though the terrorists' ethos might be I didn't think they would harm straight off *la viuda de José*.

My trust seemed to transmit itself to some extent to the girl versus myself. She sank on to the sofa with a sigh and tucked her feet up and offered me a cigarette, which I accepted gratefully, before realizing that I felt too sick to light it.

'Well,' she said again. 'How did you find us then? How did you get here? And why did you come?' A pause while she stared me for the first time straight in the eye. She was trying for hauteur but it didn't really work. 'Did you tell anyone else you were coming?'

'I haven't told the police, if that's what you mean,' I said, shelving the other questions for the time being and staring back at her.

She laughed – a dry unamused laugh which turned to a cough in the wake of errant cigarette smoke: I doubted she was really a smoker at all, it was just part of the act. 'Of course I don't mean the police,' she said. 'If you intended to tell the police you wouldn't be here, would you? You couldn't be, not very well.'

Couldn't I? I knew it was absurd and that no one was likely to believe me, but this was the first time I realized in full the gravity of what I was doing, and what I had already done. Had I gone straight to the police the way I should, this *covo* or whatever the place was called would have been surrounded hours back, and its inhabitants safely arrested. Now, thanks to me, they would have time to escape. Which made me – what? Their accessory? Their accomplice? Yes, probably their accomplice. Ah well, too late now to worry about things like that. 'I shall tell them though,' I said, blushing on account of my rectitude. I felt horribly prim – Girl-Guidey. The girl's transgressiveness was so much more alluring; small wonder Lorenzo had found it so, too. Maria Schneider versus Julie Andrews: no contest at all. 'I shall tell them the moment I'm out of this place. I'll have to.'

'Ah.' The news didn't seem to surprise her or even affect her much. She took another drag on the cigarette – a more practised one this time – and settled back among the incongruous cushions. 'It makes no difference anyway,' she said. 'Sooner or later we'd have had to leave this flat. It's too exposed, it's never been much use to us.'

It must have been handy for Lorenzo though, so close to home. I wondered if he'd chosen it and if he'd paid the rent.

As if reading my mind the girl winced slightly. Or perhaps I just imagined it. 'José never spoke about things to you, did he?' she asked in a slightly less confident tone of voice. 'I mean, that wasn't how you found your way here, was it? Through something he told you, or maybe let slip . . .'

I toyed with the idea of claiming more knowledge than I in fact possessed, just to disorient her, reverse for a moment our positions of confidante and outsider, but decided the truth would work every bit as well. Stressing the 'Lorenzo' – the José nonsense both angered and disgusted me – I explained in full the story of the photograph.

She received it at first in dumbfounded silence and then began protesting that it couldn't be so, that I must have made it up. 'José couldn't have done anything so stupid, so unprofessional! I can't believe it of him! *Keep* the thing? Keep the photograph? Why, if the police had found it we'd have been netted on the spot. How could he have done a thing like that? How could he, how could he?'

In the same way that he blew himself sky high, I wanted to reply, but was stopped by the sudden entry of a youngish man in a black rayon track suit, who had evidently been following the conversation from the next room. The bridegroom in the wedding shot.

'Signora Gherardi,' he drawled in an exaggeratedly polite accent, staring at me hard with his head on one side. It wasn't a question, still less a greeting, it was a statement of fact and as such I answered it.

'Yes.'

'The grieving widow.'

This second label rang more like a provocation. The man was looking at me in a funny way, too: challengingly, as if he expected some kind of reaction that I wasn't providing. I returned his stare: in the picture the face had seemed familiar but in the flesh, no, it was that of a total stranger.

'Yes,' I said again flatly. 'Yes, my husband is dead all right, and yes, I still miss him.'

My attempt at dignity was lost on him. For some reason he disliked me intensely already. 'Don't we all?' he replied. 'I miss him for one. The organization misses him. And Roberta here,' and he laid a finger on the girl's shoulder and prodded her forward briskly, almost sharply, 'she misses him, too. Don't you, Robbie? Go on, tell Signora Gherardi how much you miss our fallen comrade.'

It was so obviously done, and with such an obvious purpose, that although I'd worked out already on my own account how things stood between Lorenzo and the girl, I was shocked.

What had I done to stir up such malice in someone I'd only known for fifteen seconds or whatever it was? I simply couldn't imagine. Except that perhaps I could, because the skin antipathy, if that was the name for it, was beginning to work both ways. Now that I inspected the chap properly it struck me I had never seen anyone so ugly yet at the same time so insignificant. Those bulgy, watery eyes and that dry beige hair that looked as if it'd been pilfered from a taxidermist's waste basket, and the narrow sloping shoulders and receding chin . . . Wait, perhaps that was it: envy of Lorenzo that extended itself to me. Perhaps he'd been keen on this girl, this Roberta creature whose husband he was impersonating, and had resented the easy way Lorenzo had carried her off. Or no, perhaps it was no pretence, perhaps he and the girl were really man and wife, and . . .

Too many hypotheses, too complicated to work out. And anyway, besides paining me, the personal questions were not what really interested me. I didn't give a damn for this unlikely couple's sex lives, nor how far or in what way they had intertwined with Lorenzo's. Shouldn't, mustn't, wouldn't. Hell to all that. Like Paolo I wanted to find out what made them tick.

The girl's machinery I decided I could already figure out. A little, anyway. She was yielding, everything about her said as much. A follower. A romantic. It would be the life, not the creed, that had seduced her. The life and – yes, probably the looks and persona of my cheating Che Gherardi as well. She wouldn't have quibbled over words with him: she would have opened her sultry mouth and drunk them all in. Imperialist aggression, conspiracy of the multinationals, alienation of the workforce, even the wretched fetishism – gloo, gloo, gloo, down that pretty smooth throat they would have all gone. Together with . . .

But I couldn't bear touching on that side of things: not the nearness of the two of them, not the caresses they had exchanged, not the picture of Lorenzo's body hunched over hers at the height of his desire, or the look on his face as his surrendered fluid shot into her. A shocking thing to say, but in fact it was easier to imagine it in pieces in the morgue. Oh hell and blazes, I was going to have to find some way of dealing with this retroactive jealousy, it was a real killer. No Lorenzo to water it down for me either, tell me it had been nothing, a fling, a passing fancy, and that I was the one he had always, bla, bla, bla . . . Stash it away, that was right; fix my mind, like I intended, on the politics. If only I'd been unfaithful myself I'd have had a kind of insurance policy to draw on against this kind of humiliation, but I never had, more fool me, so there, I just had to take it on board. The narrator of *Brideshead Revisited*, which I'd recently been reading, said that his cuckold's horns made him feel like the lord of the forest: good for him, mine just made me feel like a silly cow.

I half expected a moo to come out when next I spoke, but luckily it didn't, luckily I sounded rather authoritative. Ignoring the girl deliberately I turned to Gooseberry Eyes, who had plonked himself down on a chair opposite mine, and began questioning him about what he had called the organization. Not about plans or strategy, obviously – I knew I wouldn't get a word out of him on things like that and they were not what interested me anyway – but about aims, theory, what if I hadn't found the word so jarring in the context I would have called ideals. The questions, in short, that Paolo would have put to his prisoner in the cave, and that I had been putting to Lorenzo ever since I'd had the brilliant idea of opening the croquet set. (Anyone for croquet? The one question I should never have asked. But knowledge is like the march of science: you can't jam it into reverse, or wish a discovery, lethal though it is, undiscovered.)

I kept my queries very general, having suddenly discovered that I didn't want anything about myself to emerge in the process. By the way he looked at me – probing, scathing, resentful, anything but neutral – I had the impression this

169

man already possessed quite a bit of information on my account. More than was natural in the circumstances; far, far more than was comfortable. Had Lorenzo spoken about me to him, I wondered? Complained about me maybe? Somehow I thought it unlikely: when you lead a double life you need to keep the strands separate, surely. I doubted bigamists went on about one wife when in the company of the other, and I reckoned for terrorists it would be much the same. Only more so, because they had to keep up the freedom-fighter image: urban jungle, guerrilla warfare, borrowed beds, snatched meals and all the rest. Very deflating to have to admit you are going back to Parioli to pick up your son from swimming lessons and on to dinner with friends.

I must have used the word terrorist in one of my questions, as Gooseberry Eyes pounced on it and threw it back at me angrily. A good thing really; it got him going; so far he'd just sat there, registering each question in silence and smiling a supercilious little smile. What nonsense this woman talks. How could one of our best elements ever have got involved with her?

'Terrorists,' he said. 'Get this straight for a start, Signora Gherardi.' (Like Carosi he had the ability to make my name sound like an affront.) 'We are not terrorists, and neither was your husband. We are revolutionaries. Revolutionaries in a state of war, that is what we are. If you fail to understand that, then it's no use our continuing this conversation, we would be speaking different languages.'

I didn't say so, but I suspected we already were speaking different languages. In fact I suspected that the use of a private language played a key part in everything this group of people did. I hadn't worked it out properly, it would take time and thought to do so, but it came to me in a flash that it was something I had already noticed in Lorenzo: the

170

capacity to cloak things, fudge things over with language, put things in such a way that the speaker never need tell himself outright what he was doing. In the days of the student protests, for example, *alzare il tenore dello scontro*, or 'raising the tenor of the dispute', had meant in factual terms lamming into the police with stones or bits of furniture or anything that came to hand, as did the vaguer 'to express a counter-power', or *esprimere un contropotere*, or the fuzzier still 'to pass from the plain of the imaginary to that of the politically concrete'. Members in disagreement with this or any other policy were not pushed out of the Movement, the Movement 'restructured its base', that was all. And the splinter group went off to 'create a new platform for the political mediation of historical force factors, more in line with the needs of today's productive society'. Italian, like German, was very useful in that respect. Which perhaps, come to think of it, was why Italy and Germany were the countries that threw up the most terrorists – sorry, revolutionaries.

Lord! I was beginning to sound to myself like Carosi. My next question in fact was exactly of the sort he would have asked. (Although perhaps not: I doubt he would have drawn much difference between terrorists and revolutionaries. In the relatively cushy Italian context I wasn't sure I did either, not enough to justify bloodshed.) 'Where is the revolution?' It came out bluntly. 'I don't see any revolution. Who's taking part in it besides yourselves?'

The girl sighed, as if pitying me, but I paid no attention.

The man didn't sigh, he responded excitedly, unheeded spittle forming in clusters in the corners of his mouth as he spoke. Like Berlinguer. Only there the resemblance stopped. 'The revolution is at the gates,' he said. *E alle porte.* 'It's an industrial revolution, but not of the creeping kind that took place in your country. Oh, no, this time it's not going to creep, it's going to burst out of the factories like a fireball. They're ready, kindled; the workers are ready and all we have to do is to a strike a match and . . . *Phiuuu!*'

His hands – beautiful hands, the only nice thing about him – made a splaying gesture. It looked rehearsed, as if it were part of a routine he went through often.

It also looked as if there was plenty more to come, so I interrupted him before he could launch into the rest. 'Did Lorenzo believe that?' I asked.

'Lorenzo?' (There you were: repetition. My interrogations had indeed taught me something useful.) 'Lorenzo?' (Twice, too. Plus a pause. Now he'd have to fall back on honesty.) 'No. No, Lorenzo didn't believe it. He believed just the opposite, that we were on the brink of a right-wing take-over that had to be thwarted, whatever the cost. But to all practical ends it was the same, don't you see, it made no difference. We were agreed on the necessity for action. With the parliamentary Left stuck as it is in the grip of rigor mortis, and the intellectual vanguard choking itself to death on theory, what other options . . .'

Here came the set piece that I had been awaiting. I tried to follow carefully, but found that my initial impression was right: the words were made so as not to be understood, not to be translated into reality. Years later, long after I'd discovered who he was, I would see the very same man, on television, repeating to the interviewer the same frenzied rigmarole – defining violence as the 'bones' of human intercourse and all other means as 'flesh and flab', dismissing killing as 'a normal operative necessity', defending the ghastly carnage that had resulted from this verbal chicanery as 'the most efficient way to strike at the heart of the state' – and then suddenly, as the interviewer brought him up short with a personal question about one of the victims, breaking down completely and sobbing into the camera like a child.

It was terrible to watch. The awakening of a sleepwalker who is told he has shot, say, an entire bus full of tourists by mistake during his snooze: even the greedy eye of the camera had to turn aside in shame.

Only it wasn't by mistake, and the number of victims slaughtered by the Red Brigades once they got into their stride, it would have taken a train to carry, not a bus. The full tragedy lay as yet in the future, however. I had neither the interviewer's knowledge nor his bridging abilities. And to tell the truth even the will to know, which had sent me on this mission in the first place, was waning fast. I'd thought I'd wanted to discover what had been taking place inside Lorenzo's head all this time, and when it had started, and how, and why, but the more his companion enlightened me about this, the less I found I cared.

Carosi would take me to task about this the next day, but in fact all I wanted now was to get out of this suffocating flat, with its outward flounces and its inner filth, as soon as possible. Lorenzo had been a member of this pernicious Crazy Gang for over a year now, had he? Bully for him. He had gone into the mountains with them, on a pilgrimage to the shrine of the partisans, and collected left-over ammunition from the last war? Well, well, well. How healthy, how poetic. What did the man describe it as? 'A thread of historical continuity, linking the new armed Left to the old?' To me it seemed a thread of madness, running through the whole darned bunch. Oh, Gooseberry Eyes I could to some extent understand: this fiction of a warrior state within a state must have provided a convenient ladder for ambitious nonentities like himself to rise through the ranks in record time. How high had he got? Equivalent of a minister or something already? But Lorenzo? Apart from the girl and the kicks, what did he stand to gain? Freedom from his money, perhaps that was the great secret: the benefits still his to use, but the crushing weight of it taken off his shoulders. Money purified, money sanctified. Money laundered in ashes, like in the Middle Ages, washed so thin that it could pass with its owner through the eye of a needle.

'We use money,' the man was now pontificating, uncannily close to my own thoughts. 'We none of us possess it. We pay ourselves a small subsistence salary each month; this places us outside the grasp of the tentacles of the consumer society. Lorenzo understood this very well. I wonder if you are able to understand it?'

I looked at him so uncomprehendingly that he must have taken the question as answered. Although it was something other than the money aspect that fazed me: it was the mixture of puritanism and criminality in the credo he'd just put forward, the moral hodgepodge in which Lorenzo, too, must have believed and on which he must have fed. Violence the midwife to a new society? Yes, maybe. In Hitler's Germany, for example, in Romanov Russia, in Batista's Cuba. But in today's Italy? A monster of a new society, that's what would come out in today's Italy – a half-dead embryo, mauled by the forceps, drenched from the word go in innocent blood. Was it possible Lorenzo hadn't grasped this, when it was so clear, so obvious? Was it possible (the question Paolo put to me on our first meeting) that I had been married all these years to a political booby? Not only possible, it was certain. And a Martian to wit, so far as my knowledge of him went. 'I'm sorry,' I said. 'It was a mistake my coming here. I must go now, if you don't mind, I simply must . . .'

Then I faltered, because the words – my well-brought-up voice, trotting them out politely in this insane context – brought me suddenly to the verge of laughter. To laugh would not have been a good idea: the hostility in the room was thick enough already.

With a sudden movement the girl swung her feet off the sofa and rose and stood between us, her back towards me. I had the impression she was mouthing something to her companion, as I saw him shrug and make a tiny braking gesture with his hand. Wait, don't rush it. Perhaps she was asking him whether or not it was necessary to detain me. Then, impatiently, almost crossly, he pushed her aside and hitched himself forward in his chair until his face was only a few feet from mine.

'If our positions were reversed, Signora Gherardi,' he said, 'would you let me go like that, just for the asking? Or wouldn't you – you know – take a few precautions?'

I took a breath and looked steadily into the ill-shaped eyes. Their owner left me cold. His question left me cold, the whole thing left me cold. (The girl didn't, she gave me a nasty hot queasy feeling, but that was another matter.) 'Such as?'

His face came closer still. 'Such as making sure, for example, that you give us a little time.'

I didn't want to commit myself. I was in trouble enough with the police as it was. 'How much time?'

'Not much. Enough to get our things together, to get clear of the area.'

I nodded, relieved. 'You'll have that anyway. My con-science will lead me straight to the nearest telephone, but it'll take me some time to find one, and even longer, probably, to find the person I'm looking for. She . . .' I nodded towards the girl, I couldn't bear to pronounce her name or let on that I remembered it. 'She was right. I can't just go to the police now I've been here; I'll have to do it differently.'

The two of them exchanged glances, and I was surprised, having written her off as a groupie, to see that the con-firming nod came from her, not him.

As I was leaving – very hurriedly after this, I confess, in case they changed their minds – the man gave me another penetrating glare. 'You have no idea who I am, do you?' he said. 'You're not pretending, you really have no idea.'

I wondered if this was some kind of test. I shook my head. 'No, I don't. Should I?'

His eyes, too round to narrow, contracted like sphincters. Resentment seemed to come off him so strongly I could literally feel it, down to the desire to duck in order to avoid its blast. 'Should I?' he mimicked in a drawly voice I am sure I never possessed. *Dovrei?* 'That is for you to say, Giulietta. I can't help you there, I can't help you there at all.'

If my surname had proved a good vehicle for insult, my Christian name afforded a better one. It left his lips like a gob of snake venom. On the other side of the door I paused a moment with the worrying feeling that I had left some possession of mine behind that would link me for ever to this place, this night, this enemy ground, before realizing that it was that: my name, I had left them my name.

Stupid of me, because they had my name already, and the link was forged willy-nilly long before I set foot in the apartment, but that was the way I felt.

CHAPTER SIXTEEN

My second totally sleepless night that summer. But this time I didn't smoke or drink or do anything harmful to myself with an eye to punishing Lorenzo; I simply sat, zombie-like but quite clear-headed, over round after round of patience, leaving the table at intervals to try Carosi's number, or else to go into Marco's bedroom and shed tears over his sleeping body. Orphan now: dead dad, jailbird mum, and furious, furious grandmother who would rail against me and bring him up in my absence to despise me.

And quite right, too, I was a fool, an idiot, one of the biggest idiots who had ever trod this earth.

To my surprise, at half-past six, when I had given up all hope of finding him and was beginning to wonder whether he'd even show up on time for our appointment, I got Carosi on the other end of the line.

I began pouring things out in a jumble, as I had done to his colleague di Guido about my find in the shed, but he intervened with an abruptness that stung me to immediate silence. 'We have a regular appointment in three hours' time, Signora Gherardi. I will not have my private life interfered with in this thoughtless manner, merely because of some wild suspicion' – *campato in aria* was the expression he used: built on air – 'that has come into your head during the night. The law is not your servant and neither am I. Whatever it is can perfectly well wait until later. I will see you as arranged at nine-thirty. *Arrivederla*.' And with that he hung up.

I was still smarting under the rebuff a quarter of an hour later, when the downstairs bell rang. It was him, Carosi – I recognized his voice over the intercom. For a second I was tempted not to answer, just to leave him standing there in the street, insult for insult, but then, across the abyss of my despair a tiny little strand of hope began to form: perhaps – it *was* just possible, wasn't it? – he had shut me up deliberately for fear of our conversation being intercepted; perhaps, perhaps my instinct about him had been right and he was here to help me.

I went downstairs to let him in – whatever his business I thought it was better no one saw him – and as I observed him through the glass of the door I thought fleetingly how different he was from the man I remembered. My head held still the picture of the fairy-story villain, beetle-browed and cruel and sneering, but he wasn't like that at all, he was just a very dark man with in fact a rather interesting and – well, yes, almost attractive face. *In* its way. Maybe the holiday had done him good, maybe it was the daylight that suited him better than the neon of his cubbyhole, or maybe it was me, coming at last to my senses.

Or my senses coming back to me. When he spoke, the whiff of tobacco on his breath that had so disgusted me at our first meeting brought with it quite another message: it smelt of masculinity.

Maybe as a result of this I felt an unguarded, slightly fatuous smile coming to my face – it was ages since I'd noticed the gender of a person, like that, on its own, as a quality apart – but luckily I reined it in in time, as his voice and manner remained unchanged: formal, distant, not a trace of sympathy, still less connivance. 'Perhaps you will now tell me, Signora Gherardi,' he said. (Backsliding? I'd thought we'd got to the Juliet stage before when we were face to face, but maybe not. No, of course not, what was I imagining?) 'Perhaps you will tell me, now that there is no danger of our being overheard and of your being whisked off to prison on the instant, exactly what it is that you have gone and done. Tell me everything, you understand, from start to finish. I can't promise any form of help, let alone immunity, but I assure you I will listen. And then we'll see.'

I think I started babbling right there in the doorway, I was so anxious to make my confession, but he must have hushed me up again – only more gently this time – as I remember retreating with him into the lift in a strange huddled fashion, rather as if he were protecting me from a storm, and ending up in the flat, in the kitchen. We were still there when Bice got up and started moving around, although Carosi left shortly after this so as not to be seen. We must have talked for about an hour – at least I did: he spoke much less. I even managed at one point to get him to accept a cup of coffee. Great triumph of intimacy: I think that was when I began seriously to believe that he might indeed work the miracle and pull me out of the mess in which I'd landed myself.

He listened to me, as I said, almost without interruption. When I got to the bit about the girl I was so miserably ashamed for some reason, and skated over it so clumsily and fast, that he made me go back over it a couple of times until I'd told perhaps even more than I intended; but this was the only time he tried to steer me. For the rest he just let me jabber. My haste, my motives (if you could call them that: impulses is the better word), my superficiality in not weighing the consequences till it was too late, the brain-storm that had come over me in the car when I knew I had

179

finally found the right place – out it all came. Despite the many stupid things I had done that night, I must have known in some still functioning chamber of my brain that it was the only way to reach him. Total sincerity. The whole truth and nothing but. Had I fenced with him, as in the bad old Torquemada days, he wouldn't have seen inside me clearly enough. He wouldn't have seen the muddle, or the pain, or the innocence-cum-ignorance with which they were mixed. Funny, I suppose to tell the truth I had always wanted from the outset to impress him as being clever, whereas now my only salvation lay in him judging me the exact reverse.

When I had finished, the weight of what I had said seemed to have transferred itself to him. I felt light, and he appeared to be bowed down with cares. He put his head in his hands as if to support it and began moving it tentatively from side to side. It wouldn't have surprised me had he let out a groan, only of course he didn't, he was far too controlled.

'Life is a curious process,' he said after a while, staring into the coffee cup. 'From the moment I first saw you – no, even before – I have wanted nothing so much as to clap you in prison where I felt you belonged. And now that you give me the opportunity I find . . .'

He looked up. I tried to read his face but I couldn't. That is, on another man I would have been able to, but on him I couldn't: the emotion I thought I saw just didn't tally. 'You find?'

He frowned and the Pluto scorn came back. 'Nothing,' he said curtly. 'It costs the state money to keep people in detention, that's all. And I doubt in your case the expense would be justified. What would you learn there, for a start? What would the experience do to you?'

I thought of Valeria, struggling to staunch her blood with

magazine pages under the eye of the lecherous warder, struggling to keep her dignity, to keep the kernel of herself intact. What would something like that teach me? A great deal probably. Yes, probably a great deal. 'I think it might teach me humility,' I said, and tried to look chastised: a little flare of gaiety inside me already told me the way his thoughts were going. 'I think it might teach me to be genuinely democratic.'

His lip twitched downwards in distaste, the answer clearly disappointed him. 'In the sense that you would at last mingle on equal terms with members of the lower classes?'

No, I said, not that. In the sense that, like the convict in Kafka's story or whoever's it was, I would learn the lesson at last on my own skin, instead of just out of a book.

'Oho,' he said, and then used my Christian name for – yes, indeed it was the first time, I'm sure I would have remembered otherwise, it made such a strange impression. 'Your skin. Yes, your skin. Well, perhaps all things considered your skin is better left the way it is.'

And then, making a sign with his hand to indicate that I say nothing to interrupt him, he took up an old exercise book that was lying on the dresser and that Bice and I used for our shopping lists, and began first to doodle and then to write.

He wrote quickly, fluently, once he had started. 'When I've left you are to study this carefully,' he said, ripping out the page. 'And when you are sure you have understood it, you are to tear it up in little pieces and throw it away. Look upon it as a goodbye present, if you like. Or as my way of making amends. No . . .' Rather awkwardly I had started to thank him: I had great difficulty reading his writing and didn't really know yet what I was thanking him for. 'No. Don't thank me. There's very little personal in it – it's just that . . . well, as I said, I don't see much point in a young woman like yourself going to prison. It's too high a price to pay for what in the end boils down to simple foolishness on your part. Foolishness and er . . .' He hesitated and brought the word out fastidiously, rising the moment he had said it as if to distance himself both from it and from me as quickly as possible, 'and er . . . jealousy.'

Suddenly I longed to stop him leaving. I longed for him to sit down again so that we could begin, not only the conversation but our entire acquaintance from the beginning. Scrap everything that had passed between us and start afresh. I wanted to know his Christian name: use it, so that I no longer need think of him as Carosi or the magistrate or the P wretched M or whatever it was. I wanted to know more about jealousy, and how it was he was so conversant with it, and above all I wanted to disclaim it in myself so that he wouldn't go away thinking . . .

Thinking what? At least jealousy wasn't a crime. No, but it was a weakness, and it was a blot. His opinion of me was low enough as it was without adding this further deficiency: stuck-up, arrogant, opinionated, headstrong, spoilt, superficial, politically misguided, argumentative, and now foolish and jealous as well.

In the hall he lingered for a moment, his attention caught by a pile of books on the table, among them the hefty Marx volume I had brought back from Montelupo. I stretched out my hand towards him in a carefully measured gesture that was in fact an offer of friendship, but that I could turn into a handshake at the first sign of withdrawal. Politely he managed to avoid even that. 'No,' he said. '*Niente addii.* We are seeing each other in less than an hour, remember. Your part is easy, just follow the memorandum I've drawn up for you. Don't act, don't rehearse, don't add any flourishes of your own, stick to what's written and don't worry. I will look after the rest.'

'Have you read that?' I asked, referring to *Kapital* which he had singled out and was now tapping at in a slightly provoking way with his nicotiney forefinger. (Nothing wrong with nicotiney forefingers either: they, too, bore a whiff of the male.) 'How do you rate it? What do you think of it?'

A silly question perhaps, but I was still reluctant to let him go: I knew this moment of closeness, or prelude to closeness, would never repeat itself, never return.

His answer was quick and concise, although with a ring of freshness to it that convinced me it was a spur of the moment judgement, not one that he had ever made before. '*Per me*,' he said, '*è Dickens senza lo spasso.*' For me it's Dickens without the fun.

So he had got a mind annexed to that finicky legal brain of his. A proper one, perhaps one it would have been worthwhile getting to know. Why was it I had never noticed till now?

My instructions were indeed very simple, and if Carosi wrote them down I'm sure it was only as a pledge: me putting myself in his hands, and now he putting himself in mine (for had I wanted to use it against him, the slip of paper would have been a deadly weapon indeed). I was to say as follows:

The previous evening I had discovered the photograph quite by accident in the back of a drawer. I had no idea what it pictured and placed it in no relationship with my husband's death.

Early this morning I had rung Carosi because I had changed my mind about this and felt there was possibly, possibly some relation after all. His angry reaction had dissuaded me, however, from pursuing the matter further.

That was all. Then, in Carosi's presence, and at his

insistence, I was to examine the photograph more carefully, and at that point my memory would come back to me. Enough of it anyway to enable me, with a fair degree of certainty, to identify the building as housing an apartment I had once visited in my husband's company, on what I had thought then was an innocuous visit to business acquaintances, but now realize must have been . . .

Etc., etc. It all went off entirely as he had planned. I was with him for not longer than a quarter of an hour, twenty minutes at the outside, and at no point did his face betray the tiniest sign of what had passed between us. Not even when we were alone together before contacting the police, not even when we said goodbye.

He left me with di Guido, and it was from di Guido, from a chance remark he made as he was accompanying me to the Questura for further questioning by the anti-terrorist people, that I learnt it was Carosi who had so far shielded me from their attentions. Not a contact of Elvira's as I'd thought, but Carosi. And I'd never thanked him for that either. Ah well. Maybe, one day . . . I'd played it all so badly, it scarcely mattered.

At the Questura I was kept far longer. I was shown a whole lot of photographs and identikits of suspected *brigatisti*, none of which corresponded to the faces of the two terrorists I had seen. My description of both was taken down in minutest detail. I was asked to listen to recorded telephone conversations to try and pick out their voices, but again there was no match, much to my relief in a way. I was terrified Lorenzo's voice might suddenly crop up, murmuring to the girl, maybe, with the hot, melting note he had used with me in our Cambridge days – I couldn't have borne that, not in front of these hard-boiled desk-investigators.

Although Carosi may well have ironed things out for me

a bit with this particular lot: I could have been asked all sorts of tricky questions, but in fact they handled me carefully, almost gingerly, more like a victim than a witness. When they had finished with me I was even offered a drive home in an official car, but I declined, so as to spare Elvira the vision of me rolling up on her doorstep under police escort. Not a booster exactly to her social image; not conducive to *bella figura*.

Instead I took a bus. Wondering as I did so whether my populist Lorenzo had ever been in one in his life, and deciding that in all probability he hadn't, and then realizing that the fact made me even angrier against him than did his betrayal. It was all I could do to stop myself shouting out inside me, Fraud! You fraud!

CHAPTER SEVENTEEN

Best to go sparing on dreams: Lorenzo always said how dull mine were, and I think he was right. And yet there's one more I just have to tell, as it belongs to that time and I think was important. Or so it felt on awakening. A vivid, grisly dream, not so much about betrayal as about denial, total negation. My denial, too, not Lorenzo's as might have been expected. I dreamed I was in the morgue, gone there to fetch away Lorenzo's remains in a suitcase, and when the drawer containing his body was opened and I set about making the transfer, I noticed to my horror that he was still, in some inexplicable and almost imperceptible way, alive.

That is, bits of him were. Other bits were already in high putrefaction. I knew the attendant was observing me and hadn't yet noticed what I'd noticed, so I knew I had to come to a quick decision. Can Lorenzo live like this, I thought? He who was so vain about his looks and cleanliness and everything? Even if the doctors manage to resuscitate him properly and sew him together, can he live as a kind of half-rotted human patchwork? No, obviously he can't. So I shovelled the pieces into the case – the quick parts and the dead – and clamped the lid down before the attendant could spot any movement coming from them, and then carried the case out under my arm, aware as I did so of the small silent and terrible struggle that was going on inside.

There, that's treachery for you if ever there was.

The mind chooses funny symbols though. The second week of September was the time the news came through from Chile of the downfall of Salvador Allende. It hit me as no news had done since – well, since my private catastrophe, and it made me feel enraged and stirred and guilty all rolled into one, and it made me fall in love again with the Left. To the extent that, despite the guilt, I knew my love had never really ceased. Left was right and Right was wrong, the equation was as simple as that. How could you doubt it when you saw the photographs of the stadium turned into a mass prison, and the faces of those arrested – just for their ideas, just for believing in equality and for trying to bring about a better, more humane state of affairs in their beleaguered land. Through fair means, what was more; not through violence, like some I could mention, but through the agency of an elected government.

So perhaps the treachery I dreamed of perpetrating was the treachery of my ideals, and had nothing to do with Lorenzo at all. Whichever way, it shamed me into renewed allegiance. I didn't renew my Party subscription which I had sort of let languish since my walks with Valeria, but in my heart I renewed my vows, my act of faith.

And maybe as a result I felt happier again about picking up some of the old friendships I had also let languish. Not Sergio, I still had so many reservations about him, but Marta, Torquato, Vittorio – I got in touch with all of them. Marta had some translating work from the English for a human-rights organization she worked for in her spare time, which she passed on to me. Torture depositions, mostly from South and Central American dictatorships. Terrible, terrible material; things to give you nightmares;

187

things to haunt you during the daytime as well. I put it all down on tape, and with each recording my lapsed faith grew livelier, stronger: the Cuban experiment was working out all right, surely. And the Chinese, and the Albanian. No torture there from the looks of things. Unless Marta's organization, which had a definite leftist slant, had weeded out beforehand . . .

Oh, to hell with it all – politics, morals, death, mourning, loyalty, betrayal, the lot. My mind had been brooding on these things for so long; it was time to let go, relax, think of something unconnected and frivolous instead. A weekend by the sea with Marco, for example – somewhere in the south: the south was wonderful at this time of the year. Or a shopping expedition: a dramatic long coat – everyone was wearing them now; even men; even Paolo, who was so short he looked like a glove puppet in his.

With something of this kind in mind I rang Valeria – the ideal companion for either outing, if her Marcello/Othello would only let her go – but I got no reply. I hadn't seen her in the park either, since I'd got back. Odd. Although perhaps not, perhaps Marcello's family were still away by the sea and he had decided to take her away for a holiday somewhere himself. With the Alsatian? Yes, why not? With the Alsatian. Or else they'd kennelled it. No, with the premium she set on freedom Valeria would never send her dog to kennels. But never mind, wherever she was she'd soon be back.

The weeks passed, however, turned into months, and still no sign. I missed her, and off and on worried about her. My dog-life was not the same without her: walks were dull and I didn't dare wander through the wild parts of the park on my own for fear of the prince and the maniac. Occasionally I went there with Franny – we'd knotted together the rag-ends of our friendship again, and for practical purposes the knot seemed to hold – but it was nothing like such fun.

Christmas came and went. Dull, too. Dull and rather sticky: Elvira was keeping up a defiant attitude *vis-à-vis* the rest of the family and refused to go anywhere or invite any relatives in. 'We don't need their pity. We are fine, just the four of us. *Stiamo benissimo.*' The word *benissimo* cropped up so often it began to sound like a litany response. She heaped Marco with presents, and he sat disconsolately under the tree in their midst, and when urged to open them, said thank you, Nonna, but he was waiting for his cousins. 'This year they aren't coming, *pulcino.*' 'Why not? Are they dead, too?'

Nicolò livened things up a little by bringing a girlfriend who Elvira instantly hated, but it was scant relief. We were all glad, I think, when the period of enforced festivity was over and we could go back to being *malissimo* or whatever we were before.

But, no, I am exaggerating. I wasn't *malissimo*, not as things stood now. I was simply lonely and a trifle bored, due to the sudden lack of happenings. Drama at least has that to be said for it: it isn't boring. It may be harrowing, it may put a sword through your heart, upset your insides, wreck your nerves, stop you sleeping, give you ulcers, but it doesn't bore you, not the way its aftermath does. It sounds daft, but I actually began to hope that the anti-terrorist squad would want to question me again soon – proof that the excitement, tension or whatever it was, wasn't entirely over – and awaited their summons with a flutter in my stomach, like a teenager does a date. Moral: I suppose you get used to anything in the end, even the rack.

In January Paolo, who I think had me a bit on his conscience now – much sweat, large bill, nothing to show for it – invited me to go the mountains with a group of friends of his. Not far away, just the mountains north of Rome; and not for long, just a weekend.

I dithered and then, virtually pushed by Elvira, who said I must, I must, I was growing into quite an old hermit, accepted.

During our stay – I don't know how exactly – I found myself in bed with one of the other guests, making love, or being made love to. It was another funny bracket time, I think that's what it was: petrol was scarce and on certain days of the week cars were forbidden to travel; it snowed, too, heavily, and thus we found ourselves – or at least I did – encased in this peculiar little quiet white world, where the rules and customs of the real one no longer seemed to apply. Isolated, sealed-off, a trifle stranded even, as if I were a plastic figure in one of those little glass bubbles you shake up, precisely for the snowstorm effect.

Anyway, whatever the cause, whatever the reason, there I was, naked and horizontal and consenting (and only the tiniest bit passive when it came to the crux), in the hands of a man again. Socializing, I suppose you could call it, joining once more in the party games.

He was a nice man, my partner. Discreet, thoughtful. Affectionate even. Quite nice-looking, too. Paolo and the others watched the unfolding of what they clearly hoped would blossom into a proper affair between us with approval, but there was one girl, I noticed, who was not so lenient. I think, without realizing it, I may have been poaching on what she considered to be her reserve.

I hope she got him in the end, if that was what she wanted, because I couldn't have done – wanted him, I mean, not the way I behaved. I am almost ashamed to relate it, but the moment we got back to Rome again the whole business faded so incredibly fast from my memory (in this truly like the breaking of a bubble), that when the telephone rang, as it did – oh God, maybe it was even that same evening, although I hope it was at least the evening after – and a voice said, 'Hey, *bellissima*, it's Sandro speaking,' I thought it was someone who'd got the wrong number and replied that I didn't know any Sandros, and hung up. I did it twice, what's more – the second time, when the voice insisted in a rather intimate sort of way that I did know a Sandro and the other way round, quite crossly: I thought it was some silly joker. Only after I had replaced the receiver did I remember my snowstorm lover's name. And by then . . . Oh, hang it, I'd really messed things up. He never rang again, poor man, and I don't blame him. A disgusted and/or disappointed silence. I have a feeling he may have said something to Paolo about me, though, as I got some very funny looks from that quarter afterwards – and no more invitations.

My life – manless, jobless, but still not calm enough really to push me into seeking either – centred more and more round Marco. It was his last year in nursery school and he was due to go to his primary in September. I did the rounds of the local state-run establishments with a view to choosing the friendliest of these, or at any rate the least daunting, and in doing so I found myself caught up in a mesh of new acquaintances, the vitality and suction-power of which quite swept me off my feet.

Italian schools were in a ferment at that time. Politics wafted down every huge old corridor and out of every rickety classroom window. For one thing the battle for the divorce referendum was in full swing (and despite the view I ascribe to Valeria, for most people it *was* a political battle, not a private one); and for another, new laws were being introduced to give parents and students more of a say in the actual running of the schools. How much of a say was still at rumour-level, but polls to elect representatives of both groups were already fixed for early in the coming year and campaigning was well under way on this front, too.

The two issues – Divorce and what was unfailingly referred to, no matter who said it or what they meant by it, as *Democrazia nella Scuola* – were somehow conflated and cross-fertilized in the minds of the adult participants, giving rise in most of the schools I visited to what amounted to not so much a pre-electoral atmosphere as to a state of pre-civil war, affecting staff and parents alike. Tension, division, polarization into Righteous Right on the one side, and Libertarian Left on the other. Catholics versus free-thinkers, conservatives versus radicals, middle-of-the-roaders versus fringe-riders, and generally speaking (for there were curious exceptions on both sides) the older and fuddy-duddier elements versus the younger and more go-ahead. In the school I finally settled for you could practically see the trenches dividing the two camps, and the flags fluttering over their respective headquarters.

The result, to a newcomer like myself, was both bewildering and irresistible. Once Marco's name went down on the register and word got about who he was, instead of the cold-shouldering I had feared, the 'Democratic' faction (meaning of course the left faction, the right faction had been slower in nabbing the name and had to be content in calling itself 'Committee for Parent–Teacher Collaboration') began to court me like an heiress.

It was strange, and rather touching in a way. Lorenzo's end was known to all of them. It must have been. End *and* coda. No one could seriously have thought he was anything other than his actions had proved him to be: a blundering, tenderfoot member of an extreme left-wing terrorist organization, dead through his own fault and probably to many other innocent people's advantage. And yet, so strong was the reluctance of the average sympathizer with the Left to believe this, that they persisted in seeing me and treating me as if I were some kind of edifying symbol, living proof of the extreme wickedness and cunning of the Italian secret services. Who must, must, must have been behind it all. Mustn't they? Didn't I agree?

Um, well. I tried to disabuse them, but left off when I saw that it was not so much unpopular as downright impossible. If I, his widow, doubted Lorenzo's probity, it merely meant the secret services were wickeder and cunninger still: the *bastardi* had done their work so well they had fooled even me. No, if I still believed in the ideals my husband had died for, I must sign up on the Democratic Parents' list and make myself available for typing work and canvassing and whatever other help I could give. Had I got a big flat? Space was needed for reunions. Did I know anyone who could help with hiring a hall or something for later on when the group grew bigger? The headmaster was such an old stick-in-the-mud, he'd never let us use the school. Did I have access to a cyclostyle machine? What about contacts with the press – surely after the odyssey I'd been through I must have plenty of those?

So, reluctantly at first, but less and less so as the sheer momentum of the thing took over, I joined the Democratic Parents in their bid for power. We met at least twice a week, sometimes more. My circle of friends, shrunk to just a handful, expanded all of sudden like ringworm. Rita and Piero, although their children in fact attended a French school on the other side of the city and were way out of the conflict, managed to get involved, too, and their flat – huge and hospitable – became a kind of unofficial centre of operations. In all I think the regulars were about seven different couples, but others came and went, bringing the total for an average evening much higher.

I don't remember many of the names any more, but when I go to visit Elvira I still see some of the faces – in the shops, for example, outside the bank, by the paper stall – and some of them still smile at me. Which I think is nice of them, considering. Three of them, two men and a woman, have since become quite famous – in the political sphere of course, where else – and them I see on television. I doubt they would be among the smiley ones, but you never know.

Ottavio – that was the name of our chief paladin, his at least I could never forget. We were all of us more than a little bit in love with Ottavio. The men as well as the women. His gift of the gab was astonishing, even for an Italian. He should have been christened Orfeo. He beguiled us at our meetings with soul-stirring visions of how we, hitherto powerless cogs in the state machine, would gradually but inexorably change the entire system of education in the country. We would sanitize the teaching corps, rid it of all the old reactionary pussyfooters like Maestro Calogero and Signorina Bianchi (retching noises here, they were two favourite butts); we would re-write the textbooks so that due emphasis would be given to the countless heroes of the Italian resistance (countless? I didn't like to say so but I thought I could count them all right, and quite quickly); we would modernize the syllabus, jazz up the timetable, get proper sports facilities introduced and influence the whole course of scholastic architecture while we were about it.

We, the humbler workers in the cause, listened, enchanted, and painstakingly copied out leaflets setting forth our ideas (our *piattaforma* as it was called, our platform) and inviting all comers to a series of pre-electoral get-togethers, culminating in a large confrontational rally with the opposite faction, to be held on the eve of the ballot. The cyclostyle machine had not, alas, materialized. Then, our attention wandering slightly, we would light up our fags – spliff was unknown to us, far too racy – and drift back to our favourite activity of bashing our foes in the other parent

194

group: how dowdy they were, how strait-laced, how out-of-touch, how pathetic.

I wondered sometimes what Valeria would have said to all this, whose side she would have been on, where her sympathies would have lain? Frankly I don't think the Democratic Parents taken as a whole would have reaped many of them, but there. She would have said, Make sure there's chalk and a blackboard first, you silly *baccalàs*, and then start talking about reforms; or something like that. Sadly though, whatever it was, I was never to hear her say it (not properly, that is, not aloud), as I was never to see her again. She had stalked out of my life the way she had entered it – nonchalantly, without a word of greeting or explanation. One day in the park I met a lonely figure plodding his way truculently through the undergrowth in jogger's rig, whom I recognized, from having seen him once briefly through the window of his car, as Marcello. I stopped him in his tracks – puzzling him somewhat because I don't think he recognized me, not until I gave my name – and asked where Valeria was and when she was coming back.

Disastrous effect. He blinked at me, swallowed and then burst into tears that sprayed off him with the sweat and on to me, and said between sobs, *Mai, mai, mai.* Never, never, never. It turned out that, with the easing of the frontiers and the changed attitude to refugees in general, he'd made the terrible mistake of paying Valeria's plane ticket to Budapest that summer so that she could at last go and visit her parents.

'I should have taken a leaf from their book,' he said. 'From the communists. They never let anyone out who's not got ties to bring them back. I should have kept the dog, that's what I should have done. Kept him as a hostage. *Cretino!*' And he began pummelling his head, thus dislodging more moisture.

It turned out that Valeria had taken advantage of the holiday to find herself a Hungarian boyfriend, with less money of course than Marcello but also with fewer obligations, and that she was now living with him happily and expecting a child. Which was what evidently she had always wanted: I remembered her saying as much once, only I hadn't really attached much importance to it at the time.

Ah well, the boiler suit would fill out nicely. I only wished she'd found time in all these months to send me a postcard telling me the news herself, and said as much to the dejected Marcello, but then, as we both agreed on parting, she was not one for formalities. He didn't give me her address and I didn't ask: I knew instinctively that chapter in my life was closed.

CHAPTER EIGHTEEN

Yes, the chapter with Valeria was closed, but there were footnotes to it, more important than I thought. She had gone for good, and yet in a strange way no sooner did I realize this than she began to come back. A bit like the rabbit Harvey – who if I remember rightly was also very tall – she started hovering over me in pooka form at odd and inappropriate moments, smiling, commenting, digging me slyly in the ribs, drawing attention to things I would rather had passed unnoticed.

She was particularly assiduous in her presence when it came to the meetings with my new group of friends. Look, she would say, just when Ottavio was holding forth on how important it was that the women in our group had every bit as much a say as the men. Look at the list of candidates: the women are all put up for the piddling little task of being classroom representatives; the only important job is being a board representative, with a voice in the budget, and who's on that list? Look. Go on, look at it. She was right, nothing but men.

Mind you, it won't last, she predicted with a shrug on another, later occasion. Give them a year or two, let the glamour and the novelty wear off, and you'll see: it'll be all chivalry then – Ladies first, Ladies first. Oh Juliet, you old codfish. This 'platform' they keep on about, can't you see they're just using it as a launching pad for their own careers? Jostling themselves into the limelight, even if the stage is only a dingy old hall and the audience a lot of silly pink-thinking parents like yourself? Vanity Fair, that's all it is – listen to the way they *talk*, for goodness sake. Anti-fascist cornerstone – sworn commitment to the values of the Resistance – why you'd think they were engaged in re-writing the constitution at the very least.

I turned a deaf ear to these criticisms and a blind eye to the lists and went ahead with my canvassing work. It kept me amused, it kept me busy, the telephone rang non-stop and it was no longer journalists. Elvira disapproved of the whole thing strongly – what more could I want?

May finally saw the ballot for the divorce referendum, which against all the dire predictions of the croakers, resulted in a resounding victory for the Left. (Not for the Left, you dolt, carped Valeria. The Left *claims* the victory, but in fact people were voting for the issue this time around, not the Party. Italians are sexy and unfaithful, they want divorce, that's all there is to it. Wise up, wise up.) Anyway, usurped or not, the Left benefited by the successful out-come, and the group of Democratic Parents went out for beers and pizzas and made a night of it, and me with them. So there. A judge who had been taken prisoner by the Red Brigades and held for over a month was freed, unharmed, and no concessions made. More rejoicing in our little group. Negotiations to free the prisoner had been very complicated and controversial, bringing us at one point almost to a split: should you treat with terrorists at all, or should you just shun them and let them do their damnedest? Opinions had been hotly divided. Now it simply looked – to those who wanted to see it that way – that the whole phenomenon of terrorism, the red as *well* as the black, might well be a put-up job, a murky brown-coloured stew over which brooded like witches the leaders of the central Christian Democrat Party, long ladles in their mischievous hands – toil and trouble, boil and bubble. I could almost shut my eyes to my own private knowledge and believe it myself.

Then shortly after the freeing of the judge, came the terrible explosion in Brescia in which eight people were killed and nearly a hundred wounded. This vicious attack was attributed straight away to the Neofascist terrorists, somewhat invalidating the 'stew' thesis, which was dropped without comment in favour of a Look-how-ruth-less-the-black-terrorists-are-and-how-chivalrous-in-com-parison-the-red approach. On either reading, however, the Left seemed undeniably to be undergoing a moment of grace, and despite Valeria's efforts to shake it my faith held firm. Firm*ish*, anyway.

A couple of my new friends had rented a farmhouse near Montelupo – Umbria was becoming a fashionable holiday place for left-wing intellectuals after a prominent trade unionist had reputedly bought a castle there – so I had summer company, too. It was a sweltering August and the pool was in high demand. Sometimes I didn't know half the people who were in it.

They're making use of you, warned Harvey/Valeria (you'd think she'd stay inside, with all that fur). Who's been doing all the typing work this morning for the autumn campaign, and who's been lying in the sun all the time, swigging your *prosecco*? How many extras have they brought along today, eh? Five? Six? All staying on to lunch, I suppose. Won't Cesira be pleased.

Cesira loved cooking for people who appreciated her food, and I didn't mind in the least our house becoming a meeting point: it made a change from last year's solitude. It also gave me very little time to think, and this was good because my thoughts, when they got going, tended still to run down the same narrow painful channels – a course of briar-lined rivulets from which there was no exit, no turning aside. Lorenzo in shreds, Lorenzo a stranger, Lorenzo in the arms of the girl, Lorenzo in one way or another lost to me for ever, out of reach, out of hailing distance, and yet still paradoxically able to wound. It was as if – I can't explain – as if the two separate pains, bereavement and jealousy, fed on each other, kept each other going. I couldn't come to terms with his death because I was still jealous of him, and jealousy is a live emotion, and I couldn't come to terms with my jealousy because he was dead, and beyond such things. In my dream I could bury him all right but in my heart I could not. I shuffled the furniture around in my bedroom, placed the bed against another wall and put a different kind of light beside it, throwing different shadows. It was a palliative move, but to some extent it worked. I changed the bedcover, too: a shame because I loved the old one with its design of moons and stars, but it wasn't comfortable any more to lie under, nor to catch sight of on waking. The famous jigsaw puzzle, which I found in one of the drawers, some of its pieces still tightly locked together, I burned.

Heigh-ho. My father came to stay for the last week of August, bringing his long-standing lady friend who he had so far kept under official wraps. That, too, heralded a change. In fact, just before leaving, he announced they were intending to get married some time next year and did I mind?

Did he want me to mind? I didn't think he did, but perhaps he didn't want me to be too pleased about it either. So I compromised between the truth, which was extreme relief, and a show of totally false displeasure by saying that if he had to remarry then I thought Marigold was the ideal person. (Apart from the name, I did, too. She was sensible, discreet, had cast herself neither as ersatz mother or ersatz granny, had played up beautifully to Elvira, who on arrival had been poised for a dog-in-manger act: no, I was dead in favour.)

I left shortly after they did – just time to put the house back to its winter sobriety. Ubaldo, stacking up deckchairs and folding away tables, said he felt like the manager of a seaside hotel, closing down after a busy season: comrades though they were, I don't think my Italian guests had entirely met with his approval. The journey back was altogether a more cheerful affair than last year's: Marco was excited about going to a proper school at last, and I – shut *up*, Valeria, this is *not* the moment – was looking forward to plunging myself into the whirlpool of the electoral run-up. More meetings, more natter, more back-biting, more needling of the *fasci* frumps. When it came to the vote, we would knock them clear out of the arena; their stuffy old candidates wouldn't get a look-in.

Bice had a proverb she was always quoting at Marco when he wouldn't leave the playground on time, or put his toys away or things: *E bello il gioco quando dura poco.* The game is fun when it doesn't last too long.

A spoilsport proverb, but horribly true. Much as I wanted to and hard though I tried, I just couldn't seem to pick up again with the Democratic Parents where I had left off. The zest had gone out of the game. I remained in sympathy with them on the personal plane – they were the kind of people I was used to, they used a lexicon with which I was familiar – but I increasingly found myself standing aside from them mentally, as it were; observing them, judging them, measuring their grip on reality and finding it slack. Valeria was a bit too harsh – they weren't cynical or ambitious, not in the way she would have me believe; on the contrary, their motives, as motives go, were good and generous and inspired by public spirit. Only she was right: their feet just weren't on the ground.

It was in those early weeks of September, I think (although for convenience I may have telescoped the dates in my memory), that I went to see a film with Rita that seemed to have been tailor-made for my predicament. So much so that I came out of the cinema in tears, without quite honestly being able to say whether they were of mirth or sadness or a mixture of both.

The last film to move me to that extent had been Costa-Gavras' exposure of political repression in Greece under the military regime. A fact which was significant in itself. *Zeta* it was called in Italian, Z. This one was right at the other end of the alphabet, it was so different. It was a film in black-and-white, directed by the Taviani brothers, and told the story of the release from prison of a famous anarchist who, during his long years in captivity, has undergone a profound political change of heart. He no longer believes in anarchy, he no longer believes in anything; he is tired and disillusioned and wants to go back to the scrap of life that is left to him and forget, and be left in peace. Only of course his followers cannot allow this: he is a figurehead, a half-mythical figure by now, an inspiration to them all. So they dog him, unable to compass why it is they never reach him or make contact with him. And he flees before them like a panicking hare, unable to explain to them his reasons. Paradoxically, it is only in this way – by a total breach of faith – that he can remain in any degree faithful to his one-time companions, his one-time ideal.

Sad, yes. And yet wickedly funny at the same time. Rita

was impressed by my tears: she had no inkling of the turbid fount from which they sprang.

I'm not sure that I did myself, really, either. Not completely, not yet. But with the coming of the new year something happened to enlighten me: something that in one fell swoop laid open to me the entire contents of my head and heart – *voilà*, like a waiter whipping off the cover from a soup tureen – so that I was able to see all the ill-blended bits and bobs of opinion and emotion that had been swilling around inside.

And then to watch, incredulous, as they ranged themselves virtually in the very same instant into a new state of order. School elections were scheduled for the beginning of February, and it was the evening of the big rally which the Democratic Parents had called together as their principal canvassing effort. (See, I am already starting to call them 'them' again.) Hired hall, as planned; all teachers and parents invited – along with non-teaching members of the staff, who luckily someone had remembered to include at the very last moment; a few short speeches from the main candidates, just to warm things up and give people an idea of the aims of the group, etc.; and then what was described on the agenda leaflet as *'ampio dibattito e scambio di idee'*. Wide-ranging debate and exchange of ideas.

The term hardly does justice to the beargarden that ensued. The introductory speeches, alas but very predictably, were long, not short, and more than warming things up seemed to bring things to a suppressed boiling-point. By the time the last candidate got started people were bobbing around on their seats like kettles on a hob, the steam in some cases almost visibly shooting out of their ears.

Hostility towards the proposals put forward? Yes, that, too. A favourite campaigning point, the admission into the school of severely handicapped children, brought down a rain of hisses, and cries of '*Demagogia!*' and wails from the staff sector. 'You try looking after a severely handicapped child when you've got thirty more in the class already and no extra help!' A plea for the school to 'open its arms' to the children of a nearby gypsy encampment had much the same effect, only worse. But the real cause of unrest, as it turned out, was simply that a good three-quarters of the audience had come there in the first place, not to listen but to hold forth themselves.

The moment the debate was declared open there was a race towards the rostrum, followed by a Hyde Park Corner cacophony as the place winners, several at a time, began to air their views before the assembly. Ottavio made a timid attempt to act as speaker, waving a list around and begging those who had something to say to put their names down and wait their turn, but he was like Canute before the waves: great rollers of oratory crashing down on him from every side. 'You've had your say, *Professore*, and how! Now let us have ours!'

Those who hadn't made it to the rostrum grabbed chairs and climbed up on them and, undeterred, began delivering rival speeches from wherever they happened to stand. While, from wherever they happened to stand *or* sit, listeners of all persuasions shouted back. Babel wasn't in it.

I stood there watching, bemused and rather lonely, despite the crush. I seemed to be the only person uninvolved in social commerce, dispute or otherwise, and instead of taking pride in this I felt faintly ashamed. I couldn't fight – not a simple left–right, good–bad battle anyway – perhaps never would be able to again: the ground had shifted under my feet; I had lost the necessary perspective.

I don't know how long it was – probably only a minute or two, although for dramatic effect I like to think of it as longer – before I began to notice a certain falling off in the intensity of sound that filled the hall. Not yet a quietening, but a definite abating, as if the energy of the various squabblers was gradually being drained or finding for itself another outlet. From several spots in the mêlée came gentler hissing sounds – calls for silence – and people turned to their neighbours with fingers on their lips. Sssssh!

A voice was speaking. A measured, steady voice, making no attempt to cleave its way through the noise by force, but relying on the words it used to do so instead. On the words and on people's ability – once they had come back to their senses – to recognize them for what they were: an appeal to reason. Slowly, unfalteringly, but with the caution of a lion tamer in a cage who knows, one slip and all may be lost, it kept going until it had silenced all other voices. In short, simple sentences it set forth the law behind this power we were bickering over, explained how restricted it was, and how restricted in consequence the power. Giving numbers, ratios, compositions of governing bodies (things that had been fuzzed over so far by pretty well everyone), it showed us bluntly how the parent/student component would always be in a minority, no matter where it sat. 'If we start off divided,' it said, 'as we would appear to be tonight, we will get nowhere, do nothing, initiate no reforms, bring about no changes, have no say in matters whatsoever. It is vital we all of us understand this, or we will play right into the hands of obscurantism. Now, as I see it, the points that have been put forward here tonight on which we have a basis for agreement . . .'

And with magical precision – I don't know how anyone could have disentangled the strands of that great ball of gabble so quickly, let alone weave a new pattern from them – it went on to give a blended synthesis of the two warring positions, showing where they met, where they divided, how and how far the divisions could be bridged. I was reminded of a girl at my school who used to plait her hair into immaculate ropes in forty seconds flat.

The entire audience listened in chastened silence. Silence for Italians, that is, who are accustomed to chatter quietly even during the consecration.

'Sense at last.'

'At last someone who's got his facts right.'

'Who's speaking for all of us.'

'Who's not a *fascio*, by the sound of it.'

'Who's not a *rosso*, by the sound of it.'

Who knows his onions. (Chickens in Italian.) Who's not *fazioso*. Who's *molto, molto giusto. Molto equilibrato.*

A woman I scarcely knew nudged me excitedly with her elbow. 'Isn't he *molto affascinante*, too?' she whispered. 'Who is he? Why is it we haven't seen him before?'

My attention so far had been all for the goings-on among the public. I turned towards the rostrum, to the figure I had vaguely seen from the corner of my eye replace the earlier speakers, and froze and blazed and melted all in one. I can't think why I hadn't recognized him sooner, from the voice if nothing else: it was Carosi. It seemed odd, when I already knew – in that very moment, I think – that I was in love with him, that I still didn't know his Christian name.

I gave the woman his surname – for the sheer pleasure of speaking it out loud.

'Lord!' she said. '*Sant'Iddio!* Not that fascist judge?'

I nodded and then shook my head, so that it moved in an arc like a horse's. I felt vain again, much as I had done on the train journey to England, only about a hundred times more so.

'Wasn't he the one . . . ?' Her eyes lit with pleasurable horror. Everyone knew my story, my persecution.

I nodded again. There was a smile on my face that must

have looked imbecile in the context, but I couldn't wipe it away.

'I'll go and tell Ottavio to do something. We can't have a *porco* like that holding sway at our assembly. Somebody's got to stop him.'

I shone the smile full on her like a searchlight. I felt so happy I couldn't really connect at all. To contradict – anyone, for whatever reason – would have been churlish. I was in total harmony with this woman, as I was with every single other person in this hall. Magic night. Lovable people. Perfect world. *Porco* didn't sound quite right as applied to my newly beloved, but I was sure it wasn't meant unkindly. The poor woman didn't know him, that was all. She didn't have my luck – my astounding, incredible luck.

I watched her disappear through the crowd and then turned my eyes hungrily towards the rostrum again. There was something quite delicious in being able to watch him like this, unrecognized, undetected. Whatever would come of it – if anything would come of it at all – the relationship between us would never again lie like this, intact, un-exploited, in the palm of my hand. It would belong to both of us, it would grow or not grow, it would wilt, it would blossom, it would throw roots or none, but never again would it be just a seed, containing everything, all its possibilities untapped.

It was absurd, I had no grounds to feel like this (although I had, surely I had?), but I leant back my head and rested it against the hard back of the chair and basked in utter beatitude. A warm, bubbling peace poured into me from my feet upwards until it filled me entirely, as if I were an old discarded hot-water bottle that someone had discovered in a cupboard and at last put to its proper use. Sounds – loud again, agitated – washed over me but I couldn't bother to decode them. Movements took place in the hall but left me sitting there detached. My only source of discomfort came from my mouth which just couldn't, couldn't relinquish its broad Cheshire cat grin. I reckon my smile mechanism had got a bit rusty, too. Eventually Rita came and roused me, which was lucky or I might have gone on sitting there all night.

'Did you see your Carosi,' she said, 'what he went and did? That was him, you know. Bastard. Interfering bastard. His kid's not even at this school, either, he's at the annexe one on the other side of the park. Why the hell didn't he keep his smarmy mouth shut. Bastard.'

I gazed at her benignly and began to laugh. I was imagining her face when I broke the news to her. 'As a matter of fact I am in love with the bastard. As a matter of fact I thought the bastard spoke beautifully and I agree with every word he said. As a matter of fact I think he's the best and cleverest and sexiest bastard I have ever come across, and I've thought it always though I was too proud and stupid to admit it, and I want to spend my life – oh, anywhere as long as he's within touching distance. And speaking of touching, I also want . . . Oh, how I want . . .' Then the smile vanished as, sparked off by something she had said that had just filtered through to me, a whole new set of problems surfaced in my mind.

If his child wasn't at this school, how was I to see him? Could I telephone him again? Did I dare? Would it look wrong? Would it be inelegant? Would it be unlucky? Would it get us off to a bad start?

And what was this talk about starts? How could I be sure anything would start? Where did I get the confidence from? From a couple of glances? From a quaver in his voice when he spoke about my skin? The thing was ludicrous. What if it was just imagination on my part – self-flattery, wishful thinking? What if he hadn't broken up with his wife at all?

Or what if she'd come back to him? Or what if he'd taken up already with someone else?

No, I couldn't ring him. I couldn't arrange a meeting, I couldn't face the disappointment if he said no. I would have to wait until chance acted for me. Unless . . .

Quick, perhaps I was still in time.

'Is he still here?' I asked Rita, leaping to my feet and looking round in panic at the fast-emptying hall. 'Carosi. Is he still around somewhere, do you think?'

She looked a little surprised, but only for a second. 'Don't worry,' she said, as concern took over. 'I know the way you feel, but it's all finished with now. He can't get at you again. Hey . . . !' And she grabbed my arm to prevent me fleeing, which was exactly what I was trying, belatedly, to do. 'Calm down. He's gone all right, I promise. He was with Ottavio. They've both gone – ages ago. Everyone has practically, and now there's no one left to help put away these cursed chairs. *Uffa!*'

All over? Not get at me again? Never again? Oh my God, what an intolerable thought.

CHAPTER NINETEEN

For the next few days I lived as if trapped in revolving doors, on the one side of which lay Heaven, on the other Hell. Half a spin, and everything was fine: he felt the same as I did, he was drawn to me in the same irresistible way, he always had been. Remember how, at our very first meeting, he had advised me to get myself a lawyer? Concern, protective instinct, even then. Remember how angry he was with di Guido over the remark about the cat food? Same again: concern, indignation on my behalf. The call from Norway – that funny note of shyness in his voice? Trepidation, worry, maybe even anguish (like I was going through now) lest my hostility towards him was still unchanged. (Oh, Juliet, you fool, why didn't you tell him then? Why didn't you give him a sign? You didn't know how you felt? Nonsense. You knew all right, deep down you've known all along. Stuff the hot-water bottle – he turned you on like a furnace from the start.) And then he saved me, didn't he – stuck his neck out and saved me at the price of his own integrity, his own career. Surely he would never do a thing like that unless – unless I were special to him in some way?

Yes, but how special and in what way? Other side of the doors, other prospect. He was sorry for me, that was all. He thought so badly of me at the outset that his conscience stung him for the way he'd treated me. He didn't give a fig for me as a person – as a woman, that is – but he reckoned I'd been through enough and learnt my lesson and that, just like he said, prison was a bit too costly a punishment, both for me and the tax payer.

Could that be all it was? Certainly. Otherwise he'd have come looking for me. Wouldn't he?

Or would he? With the way I had always behaved towards him? With the encouragement I had given? Would any man with an ounce of pride in his nature expose himself like that to yet more unpleasantness, yet more snubs? (And in his nature, unless I was much mistaken, of pride there was far more than an ounce.)

I span through these doors, rocked on this see-saw, for a number of days that in retrospect, looking up the date of the rally and that of the election, I see were only three, but that felt at least ten times longer: a full month of torment at least. There was nobody I could confide in, nobody whose opinion I could ask. No daisy, even, whose petals I could sacrifice for a fifty-fifty consultation: he loves me, he loves me not. I didn't dare: the odds were too slim for my liking. I had taken a good deal of knocks lately and should have grown humbler, but inside I was the same spoilt and arrogant old Juliet of always: I wanted certitude, and if I held out I reckoned – somehow, sometime, and pretty soon at that – I would get it.

My last contribution to the cause of Democratic Parents (and it was indeed the last: the flag I sailed under had grown such a faded shade of pink I belonged no more to their fleet) had been a promise to act as monitor on voting day. Carosi's last-minute appeal had gone unheard and there were to be two lists of candidates – left and right, opposed and divided as at the outset, if anything more so; monitoring was necessary therefore for two reasons: one, to ensure that the election process itself was fair, and two (slightly at variance if you come to think of it), to counterbalance the presence of the other, enemy monitor who, being who he was and representing those he did, was bound to do everything in his power to make it unfair because he banked on your doing just the same.

Unfortunate choice, muttered my opposite number, a Mr Bonifazi, as I took up my place behind the urns, and for most of the day I agreed with him. It was just about the most boring, uncomfortable, unrewarding stretch of time I have ever spent. Aching neck from scanning the rolls all the time, checking people's credentials; aching eyes from the same (not to mention the tobacco smoke with which the room was filled – *everyone* turned up smoking); aching back from too much sitting; rumbling stomach from hunger and then furious indigestion from the dried-up sandwiches and coffee which was all the school was able to provide. Towards evening I was so tired and cold and miserable I was seriously thinking of deserting and letting the vote-count go hang.

Then, amongst the very last trickle of voters – the booths were practically closing down and the president of the voting commission was already fussing around collecting up the indelible pencils – there he was: my sulphurous Pluto. Standing on the far side of the table, smiling down on me in a way that banished all my woes in an instant, an identity card in his hand.

He says now that I made shameless bedroom eyes back at him to get my message through, or fish eyes as he unpoetically calls them, but I think it unlikely, given the company we were in. Mr Bonifazi et al. would have had a fit. On the other hand I couldn't very well have spoken either, and seeing how things turned out I must have done something, but all I remember doing is sneaking a quick look at the identity card and discovering that his name was Francesco, and perhaps, perhaps using it in a rather awkward, unpractised sort of way that caused us both to start and look each other full in the face and . . . I'm not sure. But whatever the code, and however we used it, by the time he left the room we were, save for the physical technicalities, lovers and have been ever since.

When the news got out everyone I knew was horrified. Elvira even wanted me to go and see a psychiatrist: she thought I'd been what she called *plagiata*, or brainwashed. I doubt she'd heard of the Stockholm syndrome, the term was a bit fancy as yet, but that was what she meant. Always one for contradictions, she's edged closer to Lorenzo's position lately: wears hippie shifts – which look wonderful on her – and engages in rabid anti-establishment talk. Nicolò has disowned me practically as a sister-in-law or anything else: ever since his misfired seduction attempt he's been looking for an excuse to dislike me, and now he's found one. Better so. Rita wailed and tore at her tresses and said it was the end of our friendship (which it wasn't: Piero and she get on beautifully with Francesco, the only trouble being that they've gone the opposite way to Elvira and grown a bit too reactionary recently for his taste). Paolo was disgusted and underlined his disgust by doubling his bill. That's lawyers for you. Marco was fiendishly jealous until Francesco's son came on the scene – since when they have both of them been too taken up by their own concerns to bother about parents, which seems a healthy enough state of affairs to me.

The school doesn't bother about parents either: after all the fuss they've got us tidily back in our pens again. Marco's headmaster gave a press interview recently which he closed with the triumphant quotation (untranslated of course, just to be cussed), *Sutor, ne supra crepidam!* Pompous old codfish.

But this is neither here nor there. My father, to whom Italian politics remain joke politics, even when they involve death in the family, congratulated me on my wedding day with the words, Watch it, Julie, or this one may go the way of the last: the judge season seems to be wide open in your part of the world. Pinpointing what is really the only bleak spot in my entire life nowadays: the fear of losing this incredible happiness that chance – and Lorenzo, I suppose – have brought my way.

What Lorenzo would say himself I have no idea and I have stopped trying to form one. I reckon from the betrayal point of view we are quits now. A few years back, thanks to the stepping up of anti-terrorist measures, the identity of Gooseberry Eyes came to be known, and for some reason this discovery had a freeing effect on me. Gooseberry Eyes was Marini's son and Lorenzo's sponsor and the missing link Francesco had always sought. Not the poor maligned *arcistronzo*, as I had thought myself, but Marini jun. . . . I should have twigged earlier, I suppose: the pieces were all there: the phone call and Giovanna's impression that it was Marini on the line – she'd probably heard Lorenzo use the name, that was why; the other phone call – Elvira's to Marini – when she said she'd heard the son in the background, asking all those questions; and then the way he behaved towards me at our meeting. Obvious really, with hindsight. The last thread of loyalty, which had somehow prevented me from ever voicing my suspicions about the *arcistronzo*, even to Francesco, was thus broken, and with it my last tie to that section of my past. I don't forgive Lorenzo exactly – I don't think forgiveness exists. Peace exists: peace between people who have ironed things out to the extent that they no longer see what there was, or what there is to forgive. And that is how it is with me now: I can't feel any more that he wronged me. I think he followed his lights, and that they were on a different beam from mine and led him to different places, that is all.

The only unresolved question is Ubaldo: he glowers at Francesco even now and refers to him loudly all the time as '*il fascistone*'. But I know that in the end, slowly slowly, surely surely – like me for that matter – Ubaldo, too, will come round.